BOOTS & THE HEARTBREAKER

UGLY STICK SALOON BOOK #14

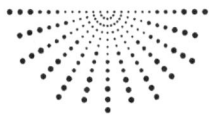

MYLA JACKSON

TWISTED PAGE INC

BOOTS & THE HEARTBREAKER

UGLY STICK SALOON SERIES BOOK #14

New York Times & USA Today
Bestselling Author

ELLE JAMES

writing as

MYLA JACKSON

For all those people who have ever suffered a broken heart.

AUTHOR'S NOTE

Enjoy other Ugly Stick Saloon books by Myla
Jackson

Ugly Stick Saloon Series

Visit Mylajackson.com for more information
Visit her alter ego Elle James at ellejames.com
Join Elle James and Myla Jackson's Newsletter at
http://ellejames.com/ElleContact.htm

CHAPTER ONE

*C*olin McFarlan stared into his beer. The pressure was on.

"It's your turn." His brother Angus nudged him in the side. "I've got Gwen and Dalton. Brody has Jessie. There's only three weeks left in Mom's ultimatum."

"Tell me about it." He lifted his long neck bottle and swiveled on the bar stool at the Ugly Stick Saloon.

The usual Friday night crowd did nothing to boost his spirits. Sure, there were ladies in the bar, but half of them were already taken.

"What about the Banks twins?" Brody nodded toward the gorgeous blond-haired, blue-eyed identical twins giggling at something Sam Whitefeather was telling them.

"I don't know." Colin cringed. "They're so young."

"Young?" Angus snorted. "Since when does that bother you? Besides they're both twenty-two and legal, freshly home from college."

Colin took a long swig of his beer and rolled it around in his mouth before swallowing. "I'm just not feeling it."

"What's to feel?" Angus asked. "You find a woman, get engaged and be done with it. Mom will be happy, she'll stop making insane threats of selling off the ranch, and we can all get back to work without worrying about having our home sold out from under us."

"Yeah, what's keeping you?" Brody, the middle brother sat on the other side of Colin. "You've always loved women."

"Right. Women. Plural of woman." Colin pushed a hand through his hair. He'd always played the field, dating a woman for no more than three dates before cutting her loose. He'd always found something not quite right about the fit, and didn't want any clingy goodbyes.

No single woman had captured his attention and kept it. Except one. Fancy Wilson.

No sooner had he thought of her, the woman on his mind walked through the entrance, smiling up at Dusty Cramer, the local sheriff's deputy on a rare Friday night off duty.

Damn. There went Colin's evening. He had just

about talked himself into asking one of the Banks twins to dance. Now, all desire to dance with Hayley or Alexis fled. How could he dance with them when all he could think about was how beautiful Fancy looked in a tight, blue jean skirt and cowboy boots?

The real estate agent, who usually wore a pencil skirt and suit jacket, and made them look sexy as hell, appeared even more amazing in the casual attire. She reminded him of that one night eight years ago that had changed his life.

The night she'd called off her engagement to his brother Brody.

The same night she'd cried in Colin's arms and they'd made love.

He'd gone from happy-go-lucky to destroying his brother's trust and losing the girl he'd fallen for. Brody moved to the west end of the country and refused to come home.

It had taken eight years and his mother's ultimatum to bring Brody back.

Fancy had left town not long after Brody, moving to Dallas to start over.

Colin knew that because he'd heard through his mother's grapevine. Not only had she started over, she'd done pretty well for herself selling real estate. Why she'd decided to return to Temptation was beyond Colin's comprehension. She could make so much more money in Dallas, and marry the high-powered man of her dreams. A small town girl making it in the big D.

A fuckin' Cinderella story.

Colin's gaze captured Fancy's for a moment. Then she turned to Dusty and laughed up at him, her smile wide, green eyes twinkling. Since she'd been back in Temptation, she'd dyed her hair back from auburn to her natural blond. The woman would look good in black, brown, auburn or blond hair. Hell, she'd probably look good bald and with half her teeth, just to make Colin more miserable.

"What's wrong, Colin?" Angus leaned close. "You look like you ate a lemon. Are the Banks girls really all that bad?"

Colin straightened and set the beer bottle on the bar. "Not at all. I think I'll ask them to dance."

"Both of them?" Brody laughed. "Might be a little hard to do in a two-step."

"Not a problem. They're playing 'Cotton-eyed Joe'." Colin pushed to his feet and strode across the floor, refusing to glance Fancy's way, although he could see her in his peripheral vision.

He stopped in front of Hayley. Or was it Alexis? It didn't matter. "Would you two care to dance?"

The two young women squealed delightedly and jumped to their feet. "Of course we would," they said in unison.

Oh good, he'd get matching comments in stereo.

Colin's jaw tightened to keep from saying anything disparaging to the women. He just wasn't in the mood for any of this.

He led them onto the dance floor, spun them both out and back into the curve of his arms. They giggled and settled into the dance, kicking their heels, backing up then moving forward, shouting "bullshit!" when it came to that part in the song.

An accomplished dancer, Colin could do the moves with his eyes closed and was tempted to do just that to avoid making eye contact with Fancy.

If having his old flame in the saloon wasn't hard enough on Colin's nerves, Fancy and Dusty stepped onto the dance floor as the song transitioned into a waltz.

"I'll just sit this one out," Alexis said.

"Thanks, dear." Hayley molded her body against Colin's and pressed her cheek to his chest. "Umm. You feel amazing."

Colin muttered something, not even aware of the woman in his arms, his entire attention on how low Dusty's hand was on the small of Fancy's back.

Anger simmered below the surface and Colin's muscles tensed. If Dusty's hand drifted any lower…

"Colin, sweetie, I didn't know you and the boys would be here tonight." Maggie McFarlan, Colin's mother, danced by in Carl Landers's arms. Dressed in a flirty white dress that came down to her knees and some brand-spanking-new red cowboy boots, she looked half her age.

What the hell?

Colin danced Hayley—or was it Alexis—around faster to catch up to the older couple whirling around the dance floor.

He caught up when Carl swung his mother way out and back in, dipping her low in his arms.

"Mom? What are you doing here?" Colin demanded.

His mother smiled up at him, deep in the dip, Carl holding her effortlessly. "Why, I think it would be obvious. I'm dancing!" She laughed as Carl drew her up in his arms and whirled her around again.

Colin whipped Hayley-Alexis around and practically ran to keep up with Carl. "I thought we talked about this."

"You talked. I ignored." She glared at him. "Now stop interrupting this lovely dance."

Stopping in the middle of the floor, with Hayley-Alexis frowning in his arms, his mother dancing with Temptation's infamous heartbreaker and Fancy so close to Dusty they might as well be having sex on the dance floor, Colin didn't know whether to throw his hands in the air, or throw a punch.

"If you don't want to dance, just say so." Hayley-Alexis smiled up at him. "We can sit this one out. Maybe have a drink and just talk."

"What?" He stared down at the woman he'd asked to dance. "I'm sorry. I need to sit this one out." Colin walked her back to the table where her sister bounced to her feet.

"Is it my turn?" the other twin asked.

Colin didn't stop to answer, weaving his way through the tables to the bar.

"What can I get for you?" Libby the bartender asked.

"Give me a whiskey," he said and took the stool beside Angus. "Hell, make it a double."

Angus sat with his back to the bar. "I don't know what she sees in him."

With his focus on Libby and the whiskey she poured into a tumbler, Colin responded. "He's not right for her."

"Got that right." Brody tipped is beer and drank a swallow before pointing the mug at the dance floor. "He's too suave. You know. He's got city slicker written all over him."

"I wouldn't call him suave." Colin grabbed the whiskey from Libby's hand and tossed back half the glass before swiveling to face the dancers. "And he's no city slicker."

"You don't think so?" Angus shook his head. "He's holding her so close you'd have to use a pry bar to break them up. Doesn't it make you want to punch his lights out?"

Colin threw back the rest of the whiskey and pushed to his feet. "Damn right it does."

Brody reached out and grabbed Colin's arm. "You're not going to hit him, are you?"

"No. Hitting an officer of the law isn't something I'm willing to spend time in jail for."

Angus's brows twisted. "Since when is Landers an officer of the law?"

Colin stared at his older brother like he'd stepped out of another world. "What are you talking about?"

"Landers and Mom." Augus laughed.

"Landers and Mom?" Colin shifted his gaze to the older couple in a clench that would embarrass his grandmother. "Holy hell. Has he no morals? That's our mother he's holding like...like... Well, hell!"

"That's who I was talking about." Angus stared at Colin. "Who has your chaps in a twist?"

"No one." Colin didn't want to admit the woman who'd come between him and Brody, was still heavy on his mind. "I'm going to dance."

"Not like that, you aren't." Angus grinned.

"What do you mean?"

"You look mad enough to spit nails. You'll scare the women away with that face."

"Thanks. But I don't need advice on how to charm women."

Angus held up his hands in surrender. "Just sayin'. You might want to tone down the madder-than-a-wet-hen look."

Colin strode through the crowded barroom, angling for the Banks twins. He'd be damned if he'd let Fancy ruin his evening of wife hunting. Three weeks. Three damn weeks before his mother followed through on her threat to sell the ranch if he and his brothers didn't have fiancées and the promise of weddings and children.

The twins were laughing at something Sam Whitefeather was saying again.

Colin didn't care. There were two Banks sisters. Sam could have one, Colin could take the other. Which one he got really didn't matter. They were interchangeable in Colin's mind.

He held out his hand to the one farthest from Sam. "Alexis, you wanna dance?"

The twin glanced up at him and frowned. "I'm Hayley. And no."

The other twin smiled up at him. "I'm Alexis, and if Sam isn't going to ask me to dance, I'd love to dance with you."

Hayley leaned over to her sister and muttered, "You won't be saying that for long."

Alexis shot her sister a quick frown and smiled at Sam. "Well?"

"I'll sit this one out," he said. "I'm better at riding horses than dancing."

"I'm a good teacher," Alexis offered.

"Nah." He nodded toward Colin. "Dance with McFarlan. He's the ladies' man."

Colin's gaze strayed to the dance floor where Fancy leaned against Dusty, her cheek resting on his chest.

"I guess that leaves you." Alexis extended a hand. When Colin didn't take it, she pulled it back. "Already on the dance floor before you get there, cowboy?"

Hayley mumbled, "I told you."

Not to be deterred, Alexis grabbed Colin's hand. "Come on. At least I'll get to dance, even if your mind is on another woman."

"Don't know what you're talking about," Colin grumbled.

"I'm not blind." Alexis smiled through gritted teeth. "You've been watching the blonde with Dusty since you were dancing with my sister."

Colin's gaze slipped from Fancy to Alexis and back.

Damn. She was right. He had to get a grip. Fancy had been off limits since they'd made love eight years ago. She'd gone so far as to leave Temptation, dye her hair and start a new life in Dallas. Why the hell had she come back? And worse, why had she gone back to being the blonde she was eight years ago?

"Thank you for dancing with me, Dusty," Fancy said. "I know this was supposed to be a business meeting. And I really do have a lot of properties I want to show you, but seeing Colin again just made me crazy. Thank you for agreeing to run interference."

"I don't mind playing the part of your new boyfriend." He winked. "It means I get to dance with a pretty girl. What have you got against Colin, anyway?"

"I can't be with a man who treats every relationship so callously. I want someone who's going to stick around, be stable and not chase after every skirt as soon as he gets bored."

"You want a boring man. Like me."

Fancy gave him a twisted smile. "You're a nice man, Dusty. I don't deserve you as a friend. I just want Colin to know that I'm over him. Hopefully, when he sees me with you, he'll get the message. Then I can get on with my life."

Dusty sighed. "Must be nice to have a girl go crazy over you." He shook his head. "Can't say as I've ever had that happen. Seems I'm always the guy the girls use to make their boyfriends..." he raised his hand when Fancy opened her mouth to protest the word boyfriend in conjunction with Colin, "...ex-boyfriends or potential boyfriends jealous. Not that you're doing that, since you're over Colin, but whatever the case, I always end up the decoy."

Fancy glanced at the man whose arms held her lightly as they waltzed around the dance floor. "I'm sorry. You deserve better than that."

"I tell myself the same, but I've yet to find

someone for me." Dusty raised a hand again. "Don't get me wrong. I'm not a pity case. I have a woman I visit in Hole in the Wall once a month. I satisfy my needs and she occasionally has me rescue her cat from a tree. It works." He shrugged. "For now."

"You need to find a woman who can appreciate what a wonderful man you are."

"Problem is, there are plenty of eligible bachelors in the tri-county area and fewer women."

Fancy's brows pulled together. "There's always someone for everyone. But you're right. You might have to date someone outside this area. Have you thought of spending your off time in Dallas or Austin?"

He shook his head. "Working for the sheriff's department, I work every shift at some time or another. It makes it hard to get to those places on a weekend, when most people have time off."

"You are in between a rock and a hard place." Out of the corner of her eye, Fancy could see Colin headed for the dance floor, a pretty young blonde in tow. "Smile, Dusty. As my fake date, you need to look like you're having a good time." Fancy tilted back her head and forced a laugh. "Dusty, you are so funny."

Colin swung Alexis out and back, and then danced away from Dusty and Fancy and toward his mother.

"Okay, you don't have to smile now," Fancy said.

"I don't think it's me he's interested in. He's aiming for his mother and Mr. Landers."

"Mr. Landers?" Dusty tuned her, so that he could see the couple in question. "I thought you said Landers was your uncle."

Fancy nodded. "He is. But he asked me not to advertise the fact. He didn't want his reputation to taint me selling real estate in Temptation."

"How could that happen?"

"My parents' generation remembers Carl Landers as the Heartbreaker." She chuckled. "He had all the ladies in love with him at one point or another and broke their hearts when he ended the relationships."

Dusty snorted and spun her again, keeping step with the music. "Sounds like Colin McFarlan."

"Colin?" Fancy caught a glimpse of the man cutting in on his mother's dance. "I didn't know he was a heartbreaker."

"For some reason, he and his brother Brody had a falling out eight years ago. Since then, he's dated just about every woman in the tri-county area. I think his record is three dates and he walks away."

Fancy heart fluttered. "Eight years, huh?"

"Yup. Though it looks as though he and Brody are back on speaking terms." Dusty tilted his head. "No one knows what caused the rift between the brothers." He glanced down at Fancy and smiled. "Some think it was a fight over you. After seein' you two around each other, I'm thinkin' they're right. Are they?"

Her cheeks heating, Fancy was glad the lighting was dim in the saloon. She lifted one shoulder. "People will talk. I loved Brody, but not the marryin' kind of love. More like a brother."

"And Colin?"

Mandy at the diner had also mentioned Colin's reputation. Fancy hadn't believed it. But Dusty wouldn't exaggerate. Fancy's chest hurt with the thought of Colin dating all those women. Apparently their one night together hadn't meant anything to him. She'd just been a notch on his bedpost. Swallowing a lump forming in her throat, she said, "After what you just told me about him, any girl would be a fool to fall for a guy like that. I'd just as soon keep my heart intact."

"What is he doing now, dancing with his mother?" Dusty asked.

Fancy turned. Colin broke in on his mother's and Landers's dance, leaving Fancy's uncle dancing with Alexis. What was Colin up to? He and his mother appeared to be arguing as they danced.

Fancy's uncle danced Alexis across the floor toward Fancy and stopped. "Excuse me for cutting in, but as lovely as Miss Alexis is, I don't want to be accused of being a dirty old man." He twirled Alexis toward Dusty. "Would you be so kind as to dance with this beautiful young lady?" Without waiting for a response, her uncle grabbed Fancy's hand and pulled her into a promenade hold.

Fancy glanced over her shoulder at Dusty and gave him a wan smile.

He shrugged and held out his hand to Alexis, who laughed and took it.

"What's going on?" Fancy asked her uncle.

"I think the McFarlan boys have heard of my reputation and don't approve of me as a suitor for the charming and beautiful Maggie McFarlan." His brows dipped.

"They don't think you're good enough for her?" Fancy snorted. "Maybe she's not good enough for you."

"Now sweetheart, I don't want to get sideways with the boys. They're only trying to protect their mother." He danced her, with purpose, toward Colin and his mother. "But I would like my dance partner back." He tapped on Colin's shoulder. "Pardon me, but I'm cutting in."

"Sorry," Colin said without turning around.

"Colin!" his mother said sharply. She stepped back and held out her arms to Fancy's uncle. "I would prefer to dance with Carl. Why don't you dance with Fancy? She's your age. Leave us old folks to dance with each other."

Carl smiled down at her and swept her into his arms. "You're hardly old, Maggie. Why I don't believe you've changed one bit since high school."

Maggie's cheeks flushed with color. "Oh, Carl. You're such a charmer."

The two danced away, leaving Colin and Fancy blocking the dancers on the wooden floor.

Colin held out his arms. "This can't be happening."

"What?" Fancy stepped into his arms, her heart thundering at his nearness. And she thought she'd gotten over him long ago. So much for time healing all wounds or broken hearts.

"My mother going out with the Heartbreaker."

"He's not the same person he was when he was younger," Fancy argued. After all, he was her uncle and she'd never known a nicer, more considerate man. He'd stepped up to the plate when her parents had been killed in a car wreck. The man was her surrogate father.

"What do you know about him? I thought he was just a client." Colin's brows dipped low. "You aren't dating him too, are you?"

She laughed. "Not hardly. I don't get into incest."

If possible, Colin's brows dropped even lower and he came to a stop in the middle of the dance floor. "What do you mean, incest?"

Damn. Her uncle had wanted to spare her his reputation, and she'd gone and spilled the beans. "Carl Landers is my uncle."

"Your what?"

"Well, technically, he's my half-uncle. His dad and

my mom's dad are the same person. They had different mothers. It's one of those family secrets that was amazingly well-kept."

"You're kidding."

She shook her head. "Nope."

"The situation is unacceptable. We need to talk." He grabbed her hand and led her toward the bar. "Come on."

"I'm not thirsty."

"I'm not getting you a drink." He hauled her past the bar, glanced around for Greta Sue, the bouncer who was standing at the entrance of the saloon carding everyone walking in.

"Then where are you taking me?" She tugged her arm to free it of his grip. "What if I don't want to go there?"

"We can't stand by and do nothing." Colin strode down the hallway behind the bar and threw open the first door he came to. "In here."

Fancy was practically flung into a storeroom filled with cases of booze.

Colin entered and shut the door behind him.

Alone with the man she was supposed to be getting off her mind or out of her heart, Fancy's pulse hammered against her eardrums and her palms grew moist. What was he going to do? Kiss her? Declare his undying love for her? Sweep her off her feet and tell her he couldn't live another day without her?

All those thoughts flitted through her mind as her

breathing became rapid and ragged. She waited for him to turn, to show her the love still evident in his eyes.

When Colin faced her, it wasn't with love shining out of his eyes, but an angry glare. "We have to break those two up."

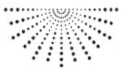

CHAPTER TWO

"Break them up?" Fancy's gaze went from confused to flashing anger in one heartbeat.

Colin loved the animation in her expressions. He'd been watching her all night, his frustration building with each passing minute she spent in another man's arms. Unable to do anything about Fancy and Dusty Cramer's connection, when he had no claim on Fancy, he channeled all his anger into confronting his mother and Carl.

"I can't believe he's your uncle." Colin spun away, unable to look at her without succumbing to the urge of dragging her against him, and kissing her to make up for the last eight years.

"Sorry. We don't get to choose our parents and family, or make their decisions for them." She planted a fist on one hip and raised her brows. "Now, if you'll excuse me, I was here with Dusty."

Colin closed the distance between them and gripped her arms. "About that… Why Cramer?"

"What?" She shook off his hands, stepped back and stared at him as if he'd lost his marbles. "First you want to break up my uncle and your mother, now you're going to dictate who I can see?" She shook her head. "For someone I haven't even heard from in the past eight years, you have some nerve."

"Okay, you have a point. I have no right to tell you who you can date." Colin shoved a hand through his thick dark hair. "But Cramer is all wrong for you."

"Why?" Her fists found her hips again and she pushed her shoulders back, as if preparing for battle.

Colin's cock hardened. Why did she have to be so damned sexy? "Does he make you hot just being around him?" He moved closer.

The sassy, determined look faded and her eyes rounded. "That's none of your business."

"Does he make you want to strip your clothes off and get naked in the back of a pickup truck, or anywhere else you happen to be?" He cupped the back of her head, his fingers lacing into her hair. He tugged, tilting her head up, forcing her to look him in the eyes.

She didn't answer.

Her tongue darting out to moisten her lips was almost Colin's undoing. "Does he?"

"Maybe."

Colin leaned close, his mouth hovering over hers. "Have you even kissed yet?"

"We're taking it slow," she said, her voice barely a whisper, the puff of air tingling against his lips.

He waited. The distance between his mouth and hers was separated by a mere breath. Colin wanted to kiss her. Based on her wide-eyed reaction, and the way she swayed toward him, Fancy wanted to kiss him too. She'd have to come to him.

Fancy lifted her chin, her lips brushing against his. "This means nothing."

"Like hell it doesn't," Colin growled, crushing her to his chest. He claimed her lips like he'd wanted to since he saw her the first day he'd run into her in town. That day he'd seen her at the diner with Carl Landers, pretending to be his real estate agent, while Colin's mother gave Carl the goo-goo eyes and practically salivated over Fancy's uncle.

None of that mattered now. He had Fancy in his arms, holding her so close they might as well be naked. His cock nudged her belly through the thick denim of his jeans, getting harder by the second.

At first, she was stiff in his arms. After a moment, Fancy slowly melted against him. Curling her hands around his shoulders, she slid them down his back and into his pockets, pressing him closer. When she opened her mouth to him, her tongue darted out to meet his.

Colin swept past her teeth, his tongue caressing hers in a long, slow glide, tasting the minty freshness of her mouth, thrusting in and out, mimicking what he wanted to do with his dick.

Sweet Jesus, he wanted to strip her naked and take her there, with the cases of beer and Jack Daniels whiskey, her legs spread wide, her pussy glistening in the dim light of the yellow bulb hanging from the ceiling.

He'd fuck her hard, until all the pain of the past eight years faded. Colin slid his hand beneath her shirt, flicked the hooks on her bra and captured one of her breasts in his palm. God, she had beautiful breasts—full and luscious, like juicy fruit, ripe for tasting.

The nipple hardened beneath his palm and her fingers in his back pockets curled against his ass. Fancy closed her eyes, her head tilting back, her breathing ragged. "This is insane."

"Damn right it is." He lifted her shirt and bra and sucked the nipple into his mouth, toying with the hardened bud, flicking and licking.

Fancy raised her hands to his ears and held on, pulling him closer. "A huge mistake."

"No doubt." He slipped his hands down her waist to cup her bottom, and lifted her onto a stack of boxes.

She rested her hands on his chest. "This can't be happening."

"But it is." Colin bent to nibble at her earlobe.

Fancy spread her legs wide, allowing him to step between. She grabbed for the button on his jeans, yanking it open with a quick jerk. Then she carefully slid the zipper down.

With nothing holding it back, Colin's cock jutted out, hard, thick and ready for action.

Fancy's fingers circled him, sliding along his length, smooth, soft and firm.

Colin ran his hands up her thighs and beneath the flirty denim skirt, pushing it up to her hips, exposing the tiny triangle of material over her sex. He slid the material to the side and pressed a finger into her damp channel.

"Do you have protection?" she asked, her voice hitching as he swirled inside her. "Please tell me you do."

"Yes." With one finger inside her, he reached with his other hand for the wallet in his back pocket and handed it to her.

Fancy flipped it open and removed the foil packet and then slid his wallet back in his rear pocket. With efficient movements she removed the condom from its wrapping and rolled it over Colin's cock, smoothing her hand over the rubber from the tip to the hilt, capturing his balls between her fingers. She gave a gentle but urgent squeeze. "Fuck me, cowboy."

Colin chuckled. "When did you acquire a dirty mouth?"

"When I waited eight years for a repeat performance." She wiggled her bottom on the box moving toward the edge, stripped off the thong underwear and tossed them over a case of Bud Light. "Don't make me wait another minute."

"Yes, ma'am." He gripped her hips and drove into her, thrusting all the way in until he was fully sheathed.

He drew in a deep, steadying breath and then moved in and out, his pace increasing with his surge of desire.

Fancy wrapped her hands around his waist. Slipping them down into his jeans, she grabbed his ass and sank her fingernails into his flesh.

The sharp jabs only intensified the sensations building inside Colin.

She leaned her cheek against his neck and whispered, "Faster."

He complied, his dick rock hard, the friction sending him to the top.

Her nails dug deeper into his buttocks. "Harder," she demanded.

Slamming into her again and again, Colin was moving so hard and fast the boxes beneath her rocked with each thrust.

When Fancy's body grew rigid and her fingers dug into his ass, Colin jettisoned into the stratosphere, thrusting, thrusting, thrusting until the sensations were so intense he had to stop. Had to hold himself still, completely encased in her pussy.

Holy hell!

She was even hotter and more enticing than she'd been so long ago. For eight years he couldn't forget her and the incredible way she made him feel. Not just making love, but being around her—swimming in the creek, horseback riding or sitting across the table, sharing a meal. She'd been as much a part of his life as she'd been Brody's, hanging around the McFarlan ranch, laughing and playing with his heart until he couldn't bear the thought of her marrying his brother.

As he drifted back to earth and the Ugly Stick storeroom, he bent to kiss her.

She met his lips with a hard, brief kiss. "As satisfying as that was, this changes nothing." Planting her hands on his chest, she shoved him gently, easing him out of her and back a few steps.

"What do you mean?" Colin peeled the condom off his cock and dropped it into a wastebasket, then folded his still-hard dick into his jeans and zipped. "From where I'm standing, it changes everything."

Fancy hopped down from the boxes and adjusted her shirt and skirt and then glanced around.

Colin held up the thong panties. "Looking for these?"

She snatched them from his hand and shoved

them into her pocket. "This didn't happen. Understand?"

Her words hit him in the gut. "Why?"

"Because." She pushed her hair back and lifted her chin. "One-night stands never work out."

"You can't say this was a one-night stand. We've been together before."

"Eight years ago," Fancy said, flinging her arm out. "I think the statute of limitations would set the clock back to zero." She tried to step around him. "Besides, that time didn't quite work out. It's not a good example."

Colin blocked her path. "What if I want to see you again?"

She shook her head, refusing to look him in the eye. "It's not happening. What happened just now, shouldn't have."

"You felt it, just as much as I did."

"It doesn't matter." She sighed. "I'm older than I was eight years ago. I should have been wiser then. But now that I'm thinking straight again, I have to put a stop to this. I'm not into hit-and-run guys."

"Hit-and-run?" Colin gripped her arms. "I'm not the one who left after we made love the first time. You ran as fast as you could, started a new life, and hell, even dyed your hair red." His chest was so tight he could swear he was having a heart attack. "You came waltzing back to Temptation, back into my life and this storeroom, and now you're telling me I'm the hit-and-run person in this relationship?" He snorted. "You've got that all backward."

"My reason for returning has nothing to do with you. You may not have moved, but you got on with your life just fine without me in it. For the record, I'm not the one who labeled you the hit-and-run guy. Any number of females you've been with in the tri-county area would call you that. I wouldn't be surprised if they have a support group for women who've been dated and dumped by the infamous heartbreaker Colin McFarlan."

Anger surged at Fancy's rejection. "Is that why you're with Cramer tonight?" As he'd made love to her, he'd never considered it the last time they'd ever come together. Hell, his heart had foolishly swelled with hope for a future together. And now she was telling him to shove off. "Are you with him to piss me off? Because I can tell you, it's working."

"Maybe I am. You're missing the point. It's none of your business why I'm with Dusty."

"That man will take any affection you throw his way," Colin said. "I don't think he's had a girlfriend. Ever."

"Don't you badmouth Dusty Cramer." Fancy shook her finger in Colin's face. "He's a nice guy."

"Fine." Colin crossed his arms. "Go out with Dusty. Have sex with the man. Marry him, for all I care."

She looked down her nose at him, her eyes suspiciously shiny. "Maybe I will."

"But remember, if my mother and your uncle go so far as to tie the knot, you won't be rid of the McFarlans. We'll be at every family event. So if you want to be well and truly through with us, you have to help me break up their little romance before it goes too far."

COLIN'S WORDS brought Fancy up short. She'd been so bent on getting the hell away from him she hadn't thought past the door to the storeroom.

Making love with Colin was a colossal mistake. Yeah, they had chemistry, and the sex was so incredibly hot she was surprised the room full of alcohol hadn't spontaneously combusted. But anything long-term with the man was out of the question.

When she'd left to go to Dallas, she'd hoped and prayed Colin would come after her. For the first few weeks, she'd cried every night. Wishing they had held off making love until his brother Brody had time to get over their break up. But what had happened between her and Colin had just... happened. The fires ignited between them and nothing could have put them out until they'd slaked their desires.

Just like now, in the storeroom. Put them in the same room together...alone...and Fancy couldn't fight her own reaction. Based on Colin's actions, neither could he.

She thought she could come home to Temptation eight years older and wiser. But one moment alone with Colin and she was the same silly young woman who'd let her libido call the shots. If she wanted to get on with her life, she had stay away from Colin. He made her body lose her mind.

Fancy sighed. "How serious is your mother about my uncle?"

"They've been out every other night for the past two weeks."

"Damn."

"How serious is your uncle about my mother?" he asked.

"I don't know." Fancy shrugged. "I'm living in my parents' old house. Uncle Carl is living at the Temptation Bed and Breakfast on Main Street. We only see each other when he has questions about the renovations going on at the place I sold to him."

"Well, ask him what his intentions are toward my mother."

"I will." The idea went against her grain. She had never interfered with another couple's romance. After screwing up her life so royally, she didn't feel qualified to butt into anyone else's. "But I'm not promising anything."

"If you want me out of your life—"

"And I do," she affirmed.

Colin's jaw tightened. "Then my mother cannot get together with your uncle."

He was right. If his mother and her uncle got together on a permanent basis, she'd be forced to spend more time in Colin's company.

"Look, if you help me break them up," Colin said, "I'll get out and stay out of your life."

"Fine." She shook her head. "I'll see what I can do to stop their budding romance."

Colin stuck out his hand. "Deal?"

"Deal, already." She stared at his hand. "Do we have to shake on it? Isn't my word good enough?"

"A proper deal concludes with a handshake."

Girding her loins, she placed her hand in his.

Colin shook it, but didn't let go, instead, he yanked on it, sending her crashing into his chest. He wrapped his arms around her and the hard ridge beneath the placard of his jeans pressed into her belly. "Until then, you're fair game."

"No way," she said, hating how breathy her voice sounded.

"Yeah way." And he kissed her, claiming her lips like a conquering hero, plundering his ill-gotten riches.

At first Fancy struggled against him, raising her hands to his chest to push him away. Instead of pushing against him, her fingers curled into his shirt and dragged him closer. She opened to him and he swept into her mouth for a long, sultry, soul-defining kiss that left her breathless and weak-kneed.

When he let go, he stepped away.

Fancy swayed toward him before she got a grip and squared her shoulders. Reminding herself that he was a player, she marched through the door. But not fast enough.

His big hand swatted her bottom with a firm slap, sending her stumbling out into the hallway and right into Jackson Gray Wolf's arms.

"Whoa there, little filly," he said.

His wife, and the owner of the Ugly Stick stuck her head around his side and grinned. "Looks like someone beat us to the storeroom. Did you steam it up in there?"

"Uh, well...I don't think so." Fancy's face burned and she hurried past the couple, noting how big Audrey's belly was getting with her pregnancy. Something stabbed at Fancy's gut. A little bit of green-eyed envy, maybe? At twenty-nine, she'd been thinking a lot about settling down and having children. Seeing Audrey's swollen belly and glowing face brought it home to her that she wasn't getting any younger. Which was part of the reason she'd returned to Temptation.

This was her home. If she was to have children, she wanted them to grow up in a small town, away from the hustle and bustle of the big city.

"And the answer is yes," Colin said behind her. "We warmed it up for you two."

She spun, short of stepping into the barroom, and poked a finger at his chest. "What happened between you and me in that storeroom stays in the storeroom. Understand? I'm not some notch on your bedpost."

"Don't worry. I won't kiss and tell." He winked, appearing to enjoy the situation a little too much for her liking.

Flustered and still too turned on to be in public, she hurried toward the very end of the bar where her uncle sat so close to Mrs. McFarlan Fancy could hardly tell where one ended and the other began. She marched up to Carl. "We need to talk."

"Fancy, darling, I'm in the middle of something." Uncle Carl lifted Mrs. M's hand and pressed his lips to her knuckles. "As I was saying, your eyes twinkle like starlight when you laugh."

Maggie smiled, her cheeks turning a rosy pink. "You always were a charmer, Carl."

The sound system let out a loud electronic shriek and everyone turned toward the stage. Charli Sutton tapped the microphone in her palm, making it squeal again, and then held it to her lips. "Cowboys and cowgirls, tonight we have a special event at the Ugly Stick Saloon. The first annual Ugly Stick Saloon Dance Off!"

The ladies laughed and the men booed, shooting wadded napkins at Charli on the stage.

She laughed good-naturedly and pointed at one of the men. "Nick McBride, I saw you throw that. You men are going to want to be a part of this dance off."

"Not a chance," Nick said.

"Dance competitions are for girls," Mark and Luke Gray Wolf called out from where they stood talking to Libby at the bar.

"Not at the Ugly Stick Saloon," Charli argued. "You will all be on the floor to win the prize."

"What? A shiny tiara to go with my rodeo buckle?" Grant said, receiving a backhanded swat to the gut from Mona.

"Shut up and let her finish. I want to know what we're going to win." Mona winked at Grant and nodded to Charli to continue.

"The couple will win a pitcher of beer."

"Eh, that's not enough to make we want to prance around the dance floor," Nick said.

"A pitcher of beer every Friday night for a year won't make you want to dance?" Charli asked.

Nick's eyes narrowed. "A whole year?"

"A whole year," Charli confirmed.

Fancy could see the interest in the eyes of all the cowboys and almost laughed. They'd do practically anything for a pitcher of beer. If for nothing else than the competition.

"Now that might be enough to make me want to tiptoe through the tulips with my honey." Nick rose from his seat and reached for Lacey's hand. "Come on, darlin'. We have a dance contest to win."

Lacey Lambert's lips twisted. "Since when are you a fancy dancer?"

"Since a pitcher of beer is riding on it. For a year." He dragged her out on the floor and waited for the music.

Grant held out his hand to Mona. "Are you in?"

"Are you sure? If you're good enough, it could be a lot of dancing." She slid her hand into his.

"Can't be worse than bull-riding."

"Hun, that's only an eight-second ride, max," Mona pointed out. "And we're going for quality, or we'll be gone in less than eight seconds."

"Are you telling me you don't think I'm good enough. That I won't last?" Grant puffed out his chest. "The challenge is on."

One by one couples made their way to the dance floor.

Uncle Carl grabbed Mrs. M's hand, and they ran for it, laughing.

So much for getting her uncle alone to talk him out of seeing the McFarlan matriarch.

Fancy had to talk sense into her uncle. She couldn't go to family dinners or reunions with the McFarlans. What if Colin married someone else? She'd be forced to watch them hugging and kissing, loving each other when it could have been her.

Colin headed toward the dance floor, bearing

down on the older couple. Greta Sue stepped in front of him before he could put one foot in the dance area.

"Got a partner, partner?" Greta Sue folded her arms and glared at Colin.

Fancy chuckled. Trust Greta Sue to make sure people played fair at the Ugly Stick. She was a damned good bouncer. Though Greta Sue was tough as nails, Fancy had known her for a long time. Behind her tough exterior lay a heart of gold. She'd do anything for Audrey and Jackson. And God forbid someone try to harm one of the staff members. Greta Sue would be right there.

"Where did you get off to?" Dusty appeared at her side, a mug of beer in his grip.

Her cheeks heating, Fancy didn't face the man. "I had some business I had to take care of."

"Did everything come out all right?"

Her belly knotted. "Yes, it did." Better than she could ever have expected, yet worse, in that she'd done exactly what she'd sworn off doing. If only she'd had a little self-control and resisted the magnetic draw of Colin McFarlan, her gut wouldn't be in a tight twist.

Across the barroom floor, Colin was hitting on the Banks twins again.

Fancy's hands balled into fists, her fingernails digging into her palm. How could he go from making love to her in the storeroom to flirting with twins who were half his age?

Okay, so maybe Fancy was exaggerating, but there had to be at least a ten-year difference in his and their ages. What did a man Colin's age see in women that young?

Someone without baggage.

He drew one of the young ladies out onto the dance floor and spun her into a waltz, taking off after his mother and Fancy's uncle.

"Sometimes I get this feeling that women don't see or hear me," Dusty was saying.

"I'm sorry." Fancy dragged her gaze from Colin and forced herself to focus on the man she'd come with. "What was it you were saying?"

Dusty's lips twisted. "Nothing."

"Good." She grabbed his hand and started across the floor. "Let's dance." She had to get to her uncle and talk sense into him before Colin did something completely stupid. There had to be a way to break up Maggie and Carl's little romance before it became too serious, and she had to do it without making a big mess of it.

Fancy couldn't go through life watching Colin with his next conquest, and the next. Or, God forbid, a wife and children.

CHAPTER THREE

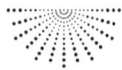

olin swung Alexis back onto the dance floor since her sister refused to enter the dance-off with him, claiming he was too busy watching everyone else to last past the first round of eliminations.

Still stinging from Fancy's rejection, he was hell bent on putting a stop to Carl Landers's pursuit of his mother. The man was no better than a snake oil salesman. Slippery as an oil slick, and far too charming for it to be real.

Which made Colin think the man was after more than his mother's affection. Stopping in mid dance step, it came to Colin. Landers wanted the Rafter M Ranch. What man with that kind of charm courted a woman in her mid-fifties? *A man who wanted to get his hands on her inheritance.*

Just like his mother said, she had full control over

what happened to the ranch. The McFarlan sons had no say in how she managed it. If she wanted to sell it, she could. If she remarried, half of everything she owned became her husband's. Should she die before her husband, he'd inherit everything, not her sons.

Angus, Brody and Colin would have nothing left of their inheritance.

Fuck!

"Excuse me?" Alexis arched her brows. "Something bothering you?"

Colin scowled across the room at Carl and his mother. "Yeah. A snake oil salesman."

"Seriously?" Alexis frowned up at him. "Are you going to bust into their dance again? I thought you wanted to be in this competition to win." She turned to walk away.

Cory McBride, one of the judges eyed him and started their way.

Colin yanked Alexis back into his arms, spun her around and executed a few fancy moves that seemed to satisfy the erotic dancer in Cory enough that he moved on.

As soon as the younger man strolled by, Colin fast-danced over to Carl and his mom.

"Colin McFarlan," his mother warned, "if you don't stop bothering us, I'll…I'll…"

Colin grinned. "You'll what?"

She glared at him. "You're never too old for a spanking with my favorite wooden spoon."

The remembered sting of the wooden spoon on his bottom when he was five made him pause in his pursuit. Then he shook himself. "I'm not five anymore, Mom."

His mother's mouth pressed into a tight line. "Good. Then you will understand when I tell you to go away."

Carl danced his mother away, twirled her under his arm, spun her out and pulled her back against his body. The man had all the moves and Colin's mother was enjoying it far too much.

Colin hated seeing her so happy, knowing Landers was probably after one thing—her vast land holdings. What the man was doing was immoral, unethical and downright mean.

"Hey, cowboy, focus on the contest or we're going to be eliminated." Alexis pinched his arm. "Here comes Cory. Show him you can actually dance."

He knew how to dance. And as much as he hated to admit it, Fancy had it right. He, Colin McFarlan, was known as a heartbreaker. How many women had he dated and dropped? Somewhere in the past eight years, he'd lost count. None of them made his blood rage or his body ignite. Not one had captured his heart. They were all nice young women, but they weren't...right.

With Cory heading his way again, Colin executed an intricate turn, guiding Alexis under his arm, back out and around behind him. As he returned her to his side, Colin's gaze found Fancy, dancing again with Dusty.

Damned if they didn't look good together.

Then it struck him why the women he dated never seemed quite right for him. One moment alone with Fancy and he was right back where he'd been eight years ago—hot, bothered and unable to control his wilder urgings. Hell, he'd broken the brother code with Fancy: *Don't fuck your brother's girl.*

If Fancy planned on staying in Temptation and wanted nothing to do with him, he might just have to move to another city. It wasn't like he could get lost in the crowd in such a small town. He'd see her everywhere. Eight years of her living in Dallas hadn't been enough to forget how he felt for her. A lifetime of seeing her in Temptation as someone else's girl...

For a brief moment, he entertained the idea of convincing her he wasn't a hit-and-run kind of guy. Brody was in love with Jessie now. He'd forgiven Colin for betraying him, and had gone so far as to give him the go-ahead to pursue Fancy again—no hard feelings.

After making love with her in the storeroom, Colin would say there was still a spark between them. Hell, a raging fire. But she wasn't ready to commit to him.

Laughter drew his attention back to Fancy. She and Dusty were looking pretty good as dance partners. Nick and Lacey had been eliminated along with

Grant and most of the others. That left his mother and Carl, Dusty and Fancy, him and Alexis and two other couples.

Alexis laid a palm on his face. "Look, either tinkle or get off the pot. If you could stay focused for more than a minute, we have a chance of winning this thing."

Colin didn't give a rat's ass about winning the contest. But he didn't want Dusty to win either. Or Carl, for that matter. It was as if by winning, the men would cement their claims on their partners. That was the last thing Colin wanted. Not that it applied to him. Alexis was nice enough, but too young.

"Let's do this." Colin threw everything he knew about country-western style dancing into the dance off, guiding Alexis with a firm, if somewhat dictatorial hand. She followed, keeping up with grace and style.

Cory tapped the shoulder of a cowboy, one of the last five couples left on the dance floor. He strode toward Dusty, swerved and tapped the other couple. Now it was down to three dueling couples. Dusty—good Lord, where had he learned to dance—swept Fancy along in an exceptional two-step, making it interesting with twists and turns.

Colin shot a glance toward his mother and Carl.

The older man held Colin's mother close, dipped her low and bent to press his lips to hers.

Shocked to his boots, Colin stumbled. He dragged

his gaze toward Dusty and Fancy and his heart stopped dead in his chest. Dusty had Fancy in a similar position, holding her bent over his arm, leaning over her, his mouth inches from hers.

No!

Colin took a step toward Dusty, tripped over Alexis and slid across the floor, landing at Dusty's feet.

Cory shook his head and jerked his thumb. "You're out, Colin."

Dusty straightened, bringing Fancy along with him, a devilish smile curling his lips. "Need a hand up, McFarlan?" the sheriff's deputy had the nerve to ask.

"I sure as hell don't." He rolled to his feet and advanced on Dusty, wanting to punch the smirk off the man's face.

Fancy stepped between them. "You're out of the competition, Colin." Her gaze emphasized the message and the double entendre.

"Colin, are you causing trouble?" his mother's voice came to him from behind.

And if he thought it wasn't embarrassing enough to trip over his feet in front of everyone in the saloon, and having the girl he'd made love to telling him it was over—his mother scolding him in public? Well that just topped off his night.

Colin spun, grabbed Alexis's hand and walked her to the table where her sister sat with a smirk matching Dusty's on her face. "Thank you for the dance," he gritted out.

Colin debated leaving the saloon, but headed for the bar instead.

Angus was there with a whiskey shooter in his hand. "You look like you could use this more than me." He handed Colin the glass and clapped him on the shoulder. "If it means anything, you were my top pick to win, until you fell on your face."

Colin tossed the whiskey back in one swallow and slammed the glass on the counter. "Another." The alcohol burned a path down his throat, warming his insides.

Libby raised her brows at his demand. "Say please."

His brows lowered and he snarled, "Please."

Libby grinned, poured the liquor and set it in front of him. "You know, dancing with another girl doesn't ingratiate yourself with the one you want."

Fuck. Now the bartender was giving him a hard time.

"Libby's right," Angus chimed in. "If you want Fancy, you have to woo her."

"She doesn't want anything to do with me," Colin admitted.

Libby snorted. "That's not what her eyes are saying."

Colin's gaze shot to where Dusty and Fancy danced, smiling at each other. What was Libby talking about? As far as he could tell, Fancy only had eyes for Dusty.

"Why don't you ask her out?" Brody prodded.

Colin snorted. "She won't go."

"She's a real estate agent." Libby filled a mug full of beer and set it on the counter for another customer before continuing. "Hire her to find you a place of your own."

"I don't need another place," Colin argued.

Angus leaned close to his brother. "If you don't find a woman in the next three weeks, all three of us will need Fancy's services to locate homes for us." His brother spun on his stool to face the dance floor. "Either go after her, or find another woman. Time is running out."

"Mom can't be serious." Colin tossed back the next shot of whiskey. It didn't burn like the last one, and he was getting a little bit of a buzz starting. "McFarlans have lived at the Rafter M since they came to Texas over one hundred and fifty years ago."

"She wants us to move on with our lives." Angus's brows lowered and he nodded toward their mother and Carl. "Like she's moving on with hers."

Charli Sutton appeared on the stage again. "And we have a winner! Carl Landers and Maggie McFarlan schooled the competition, and proved you're never too old to be a winner at the Ugly Stick Saloon!"

Every cowboy and cowgirl hooted and hollered, congratulating the couple.

"I predict that before long, we'll have a new stepdad," Angus said.

Colin's gut clenched. "We have to stop this."

"You know Mom. She's got a mind of her own and is as stubborn as they come." Angus glanced at his watch. "And I don't have time to bust them up. Gwen and Dalton are coming in from Dallas to go to the county fair with me tomorrow. I'm headed home to hit the sack. You coming?"

Colin's fists knotted as Fancy and Dusty headed for the exit, arm in arm, laughing.

As Alexis had put it so clearly, he either needed to piss or get off the pot. Either he went for Fancy and risked falling flat on his face again, or he gave up and courted another woman.

His gaze panned the saloon, slowing briefly on the eligible young women. Alexis and Hayley Banks were out. Too young. He'd probably ruined his chances with them anyway by acting the fool tonight.

Mandy McAlister, a waitress at the diner, was nice enough, but Colin's pulse didn't speed at the sight of her.

Damn. Colin hated to admit it, but he still had feelings for Fancy. Was it head-over-heels, let's-make-a-fool-of-yourself love? Hell. Since she'd arrived at the Ugly Stick Saloon, he'd done nothing but make a complete ass of himself.

A hand waved in front of his face.

"I'm leaving," Angus said. "If you're not riding with me, you'll have to find another ride home, since we came together."

"I'm coming." A last glance at his mother and Landers made his blood boil and an idea take root. Maybe it was time to invoke a little reverse psychology. He'd show Fancy what she was missing and force her to spend a little time with him working on the Maggie-Landers breakup.

If all went according to plan, he might have a chance to win after all.

Dusty Cramer might have left with Fancy tonight, but he wasn't the right man for her. Colin just had to show her who was.

FANCY SAT BACK in the comfortable bucket seat of Dusty's SUV. "Thanks, Dusty. I don't know what I'd have done without you tonight."

Dusty shook head. "Why don't you just tell him?"

She shot a frown at Dusty her chest tightening. "Tell who what?" Was it so obvious? Did everyone see what she refused to admit to herself?

"That you're still in love with Colin. Why don't you tell him?"

Fancy faced the road ahead, her eyes stinging, the pain in her chest almost too much to bear. "I can't," she whispered.

"He seems crazy about you." Dusty chuckled. "Hell, he fell at your feet and nearly picked a fight with me when I pretended to almost kiss you. If that isn't love, I don't know what is." Dusty's smile slipped. "And, for the record, I was tempted to make it a real kiss." His fingers gripped the steering wheel and it was his turn for his focus to remain on the road.

Fancy studied Dusty in the light from the dash. "I'm sorry, Dusty. You're a nice guy."

"That's my problem. If I wasn't so nice, I might have a shot with the girls. Is that it?"

"No. You just haven't found the right one."

"I'll be thirty-four on my next birthday. I have yet to be married and have no prospects." He shook his head. "But this isn't about me. Why won't you tell Colin you still love him?"

A tear slipped down her cheek and she brushed it away. With a laugh that sounded more like a sob, she said, "I thought I was over him. Seeing him again makes me realize I'm not." She looked up at Dusty through tear-filled eyes. "I can't let him break my heart again…"

"Who says he'll break your heart again?"

She snorted. "We're talking about Colin. How many women has he dated since I've been gone?"

"A few," Dusty said. "Okay, a lot. But that might be because they weren't you."

"How do I know he wouldn't date and dump me

just like one of those women?" It still hurt that Colin had let her go to Dallas and never came after her. Sure, she understood the violation of the brother code, but after a reasonable amount of time, if he'd really loved her, he'd have come for her.

He didn't.

"Why did you come back to Temptation?" Dusty asked.

"I was tired of the rat race in Dallas. It's a big, impersonal city. I was nothing more than a tiny fish in an ocean of people."

"Out of all those people, you couldn't find a man you loved?" Dusty asked.

"I thought I had."

Dusty glanced her way but didn't say anything.

"I dated him for six months. I almost married him." When she'd turned twenty-nine, she heard the ticking of her biological clock and would have married him to have children.

"But?"

He wasn't Colin. He didn't have calluses on his hands, he'd never been up close and personal with a cow and he'd never ridden a horse. He wasn't Colin. Hell, all the men she'd dated weren't the rugged cowboys she'd grown up with. She missed that.

"He knew," Fancy finally answered.

"That you were still in love with another man?"

Fancy nodded. "I also came back to Temptation to get Colin well and truly out of my system." Only the plan was backfiring horribly. No sooner had she been alone with the man, she'd dropped her panties and had sex with him in the storeroom.

"Seems to me you're hurting yourself by resisting what's right there in front of you," Dusty said.

"I don't care. I can't go through life mooning over a man I fell in love with when I was barely out of my teens." She bunched her fists. "I have to get over him."

"Then do it."

She laughed, a sob choking her throat. "How?" she whispered.

"Spend time with him."

"What?" She stared at Dusty as if he'd lost his mind.

"Spend time with him and pick apart every fault. Maybe he'll pick his nose, belch or fart in front of you."

Fancy wrinkled her nose. "Gross."

"That's the spirit. Find all those little things that make you nuts, and blow them out of proportion."

"He does want me to help break up my uncle and his mother. That's annoying." And necessary to her future peace of mind if she wanted to avoid awkward family functions.

"Then do it. Join forces. Maybe too much togetherness will breed contempt, and you will both part amicably."

She *had* promised to help him with the Carl and Maggie issue. "It might work." An image of Colin's face as he'd thrust into her in the storeroom and the resurgence of her own desire at the way her pussy still tingled threatened to derail her mission before she'd made it out of the chute.

She just had to meet him in more public places, never be alone with him and keep her panties on!

CHAPTER FOUR

"*H*as anyone seen Mom today?" Colin asked the next afternoon as he entered the house through the back door. He'd been at one of his construction sites, checking on the progress of the finish carpenters applying baseboards and crown molding in the historic Victorian house he was remodeling for Judge Stephens. They were a week behind schedule and the judge was due back from vacation soon.

"She was here at breakfast this morning." Brody's fiancée, Jessie, stood at the stove, stirring onions and hamburger meat in a skillet.

His brother Brody was filling a large pot with water at the sink. "She said something about having a meeting at the diner and not to count on her for supper."

"Will you be staying?" Jessie asked. "I'm making spaghetti."

Colin sniffed the air. "Smells good."

Jessie's eyes narrowed. "I'll have you know, I haven't burned anything in over a week."

Colin laughed. "You'll make a fine cook, if you keep this up."

"I'm better with horses," she muttered. "But I'm learning from the best."

"Mom." Colin sighed. "Think she'll be on strike forever?"

"I wouldn't be here if she wasn't," Jessie reminded him. "And I really am getting better at cooking."

Brody slipped his arms around her and nuzzled her neck. "And you're even better in bed."

"Seriously, Brody. Couldn't you wait until I left the room?" Colin turned away and would have walked out.

"Angus told me what happened with you and Fancy last night, after I left early."

Brody's words made Colin stiffen. How did Angus know about Colin and Fancy having sex in the storeroom?

"I'd have paid good money to see her expression when you fell flat on your face in front of her." Brody chortled. "Way to make a good impression on the woman after eight years."

Colin's shoulders relaxed. He was still getting used to being on friendly terms with Brody after their estrangement. His brother bore a grudge against Colin for eight long years, refusing to speak or be in the same state with him for more than a couple of days.

Now that he was home for good, and in love with Jessie, they were almost back to being like they were before Colin had slept with Fancy.

Yeah, it was a twisted story, with lots of hard feelings, but they were getting past that.

Colin shot a wry smile over his shoulder at his brother. "It wasn't my best performance."

Brody pinned him with a glance. "So how long is it going to take for you to go after Fancy?"

Jessie nudged him in the belly. "Isn't that Colin's business?"

Brody hugged her against his side. "Not really. He needs to get on the ball. Time is passing far too quickly."

Colin's eyes narrowed.

"For what?" Jessie asked. "If Colin wants Fancy, he should take his time and treat her right."

"He doesn't have much time." Brody raised his eyebrows in silent challenge to Colin.

Nothing like his brothers applying pressure to the last single McFarlan man standing.

"Three weeks should be plenty if the woman's willing and Colin plays his cards right." Jessie pinched Brody. "Now let go of me so I can stir the sauce."

Brody released Jessie and strode toward Colin. "Less than three weeks," he corrected.

"Are you sure you're okay with…you know?" Though Brody had told him to go for Fancy, it was still too new for Colin to believe it.

"He's okay with it, Colin," Jessie answered for Brody. "I know all about what happened between you, Brody and Fancy. Brody fessed up about it."

Brody grinned. "I can't keep much from this woman. She sees right through me."

"She's a keeper." Colin winked when Jessie shot a glance over her shoulder.

"Yeah, and you need to find your keeper too. If it's not Fancy, keep looking." Brody's voice lowered. "But make it soon."

Colin glared at his brother. "Don't push."

Brody raised his hands. "Fine. I won't say another word. Angus and I have the women we love. No matter what happens, we'll be fine. But we'd be even better if you could find someone of your own."

Rub it in, Brody. Rub it in.

Colin showered and changed into clean jeans and boots. He tossed on one of his nicer button down shirts and topped it with his best cowboy hat. Satisfied he looked decent, he headed for town. He hoped to find Fancy and implement his plan to win her over, while breaking up the disaster of Carl Landers getting his hands on the ranch and breaking his mother's heart.

TWENTY MINUTES later he entered PJ's Diner and stopped short. The two women foremost in his mind sat huddled over a table in the far corner.

Fancy was pointing at a stack of papers and talking, while his mother leaned over the documents, nodding occasionally and asking questions.

What the hell?

Colin strode across the diner and stopped in front of the table, forcing a smile. He couldn't really win over Fancy if he joined them frowning, now could he?

"Well, I didn't expect to see you two together. What's the occasion?" he asked.

His mother's cheeks warmed and she laid her arms over the papers on the table. "We just happened to bump into each other and decided to have lunch. Didn't we, dear?" She glanced at Fancy with an expectant smile.

Fancy nodded. "Why yes, of course."

"Lunch would have been hours ago. It's almost dinner time."

His mother glanced at her watch and her eyes widened. "Good grief! Time flies." She shoved the papers into her voluminous purse and closed it before Colin had a chance to see what they were. "I'm sorry, but I have to leave. I promised a friend we'd meet at the fair in an hour and a half." She patted her hair, her cheeks rosy. "I have to get back to the house and change. I'll be late if I don't get moving." Colin's mother leaned across the table and patted Fancy's hand. "Thank you for talking with me. I'll think about everything you said and let you know my decision soon."

"Take your time, Mrs. McFarlan."

"Oh, pooh. Call me Mrs. M. Jessie calls me that, and I kind of like it." She scooted out of the booth seat, stood and faced Colin. "Did you want something, dear?"

His brows descended. The women were keeping secrets from him. "To know what's going on."

His mother patted his face. "Nothing you need fret about. You have enough to worry about on your own, don't you?" His mother winked at Fancy. "Don't let him be a grump to you. He really is the most charming of my three sons."

"Thank you, Mrs. M. I think I can handle him. You'd better hurry, or you'll be late."

Her eyes sparkling, Colin's mother flashed a grin. "It wouldn't hurt for him to wait a while. A girl needs to play a little hard to get."

Colin's jaw dropped. He couldn't believe those words had come out of his mother's mouth.

"Really, Colin. I'm old. Not dead." She left the diner smiling, a stunned son spinning in her wake.

FANCY CHUCKLED at the shock on Colin's face. "I've never seen your mother so animated. Cut her some slack."

He turned, his brows dipping low. "She's talking about playing hard to get with your uncle."

"I know." Her fingers drummed on the table. "What are we going to do about it?"

Colin slid onto the bench across from her. "Break them up."

"And how do you propose we do that?"

"Never leave them alone, for one."

"That will be hard to do. We'd have to stalk them. Isn't there a law against that?"

"Who cares? She's my mother."

"And my uncle." Fancy stared across the table at him. "So what's the plan?"

"You heard my mother. She's meeting him at the fair in an hour and a half. We will be there to make sure they're never alone. If they decide to go out for a late dinner, we invite ourselves along."

"And if they decide to go to Lover's Lane?"

"We follow them to make sure that's where they're going and call Dusty to buzz by and break it up. The sheriff's department has always done the job."

"Except for one night I seem to recall," Fancy whispered.

"What was that?"

"Nothing." She faked a happy smile. "So what time are you picking me up for the fair?"

"If you need to change, I can follow you home and wait."

Her heart skipped several beats and made up by thumping hard against her ribs. "No need to follow me. My Jeep is right outside. I'll drive myself. Why don't we meet at the fair in one hour? You know, get the jump on the old folks."

"I'd rather pick you up at your place, so we don't have two vehicles to deal with later."

"Come by in an hour. I'll be ready." She scooted across the seat.

Colin slid across as well and stood at the same time she did, putting them a lot closer than Fancy anticipated.

She took a hasty step backward and nearly fell.

A big, callused hand reached out, grabbed her arm and yanked her against a solid wall of muscles.

Her breath lodged in her lungs, refusing to move in or out, Fancy planted her hands on Colin's chest, prepared to push him away.

"Umm. You smell like spicy apple pie." Colin leaned close and sniffed her neck. "A la mode."

"I like apple pie and ice cream. So?" Her words came out of her mouth in little more than a whisper. Unable to breathe with him so close, she couldn't expect more.

"I like apple pie and ice cream too."

Remembering what Dusty had said, Fancy concentrated on finding fault in Colin. She sniffed, hoping he smelled awful of sweat or horse manure. Instead, his cologne made her core tighten and her fingers curl into his shirt. Damn. This was going to be hard.

"Uh. If we're going to the fair, I need to go home and change into something casual." A pencil skirt, suit jacket and high heels wouldn't be at all practical walking through the grass.

"I like what you're wearing."

"Yeah, but when I'm rocking on the Ferris wheel, it's nice to know the folks waiting on the ground aren't getting an eye full of my underwear."

"Okay. I wouldn't want to share that with them, anyway."

"It's not like *you're* going to see them. I told you. We're not a thing. The only reason we're going to the fair together is to interfere with your mother and my uncle's budding romance." She pointed at him. "Hands off."

He held up his hands in surrender. "Whatever you wish."

Fancy stared at him with narrowed eyes. "I don't trust you." Worse. She didn't trust herself. Now that she'd thrown down the gauntlet for him to remain hands off, she couldn't think past those hands on her body.

Well, crap. The best way to combat her own urges

was to deal with Colin the same way they planned on dealing with Maggie and Carl.

Never let them be alone together.

She repeated that mantra all the way to her house and almost had herself convinced. That is, until she stripped out of her skirt suit and stood in her bra and panties, looking at the clothes in her wardrobe. The cool breeze from the air conditioner feathered across her heated skin, reminding her that she was nearly naked.

If she'd let Colin come to her house with her, he would be waiting out in the living room. All she would have to do was walk out there in her bra and panties and nature would take its course. *Oy!* Talk about stirring the juices.

No amount of cool air could chill her rising desire at just the thought of standing naked in front of Colin. What she needed was to slake her thirst with BOB, her battery-operated boyfriend. One orgasm coming up!

Slipping out of her bra and panties, she lay on the bed and opened the drawer to her nightstand. Fancy removed the smooth, shiny dildo from the cloth bag, applied a generous dollop of gel to it. Her pussy was already wet from thinking about Colin and their raw sex among the whiskey and beer the night before.

Yeah, she could easily take the edge off before seeing Colin and have no issues with wanting to jump his bones and make mad, crazy monkey sex with him.

She flipped the switch on BOB. He buzzed to life, vibrating in her palm.

Oh, yes.

As she touched BOB to her entrance, the vibrations slowed.

Low batteries? Bad connection?

Fancy shook BOB and he revved up for a second, then died all together.

"Fuck!" Naked and horny, Fancy leaped from the bed and scoured the house for spare batteries. She hadn't been back long enough to accumulate much in the way of spares. As she raced through the house, ducking past the open blinds, she realized it was a hopeless cause.

Back in the bedroom, she stared at BOB. "You picked a fine time to die on me, dude. But I don't have to have the vibration to make me happy. I can get there without it."

She lay down again on the bed, reapplied the gel and willed herself to relax and enjoy her self-stimulation.

Closing her eyes, she touched the tip of the lifeless BOB to her pussy, now drier from her race around the house looking for batteries. Not to be deterred, she rubbed BOB in and around her entrance, spreading the gel to ease him into action.

When she had enough lubricant to make the glide

easier, she eased BOB into her channel and the comparison began…

BOB was narrow, metallic and cold, unlike Colin's thick, velvety smooth, warm cock. She could put BOB in her mouth, but it just wouldn't be the same as sucking the come out of Colin's dick.

She couldn't expect BOB to measure up to Colin. Why hadn't she gotten a bigger dildo when she'd bought BOB? And those rubber glove things that slipped over the metal rod. They would have made the experience more realistic.

In and out, she thrust BOB. With her eyes shut tightly, she imagined it was Colin, leaning over her, bending down to capture one of her nipples between his lips. With her free hand she plumped her breast and pinched the tip.

Fancy was determined to do this. She'd pleasured herself before, eliciting a full orgasm more than one time. Now was no different.

Except she'd made love to a live, well-hung, warm and sexy man the night before.

After ten minutes of concentrated effort, she admitted defeat. No amount of thrusting, titty pinching and nubbin flicking was going to do it for her when she could have had a real man instead by giving in to her lust and allowing Colin to come home with her.

Her doorbell rang, yanking her out of her frustrated state to sit upright in her bed. She glanced at the clock on her nightstand. Only twenty minutes had passed since she'd left Colin at the diner.

Could it be? Had he disregarded her instructions to wait an hour before coming to pick her up?

Her pussy clenched and she rolled off the bed. She ran to her dresser and unearthed a sheer, baby blue robe that only came down to mid-thigh and didn't do much to hide her naked form beneath.

Colin was just what she needed at that moment, and to hell with her self-inflicted promise to rid her system of the man. Her pussy practically ached for him.

"Coming!" Fancy raced to the door and flung it open.

A man wearing a local cable company uniform took one look at her and his jaw nearly dropped to his knees. "Uh...uh..." He gulped and tried again, his eyes getting wider as his gaze swept over her nearly naked body. "Am I catching you at a bad time?" he squeaked.

Her face flamed and she covered the important parts with her arms and crossed her legs. "No, no. I need the cable installed, if you could wait just a minute." She slammed the door in his face and leaned her back against it, her knees shaking.

"Oh. My. God." Never had she been more mortified. And that poor cable guy!

Fancy pushed away from the door and ran for her bedroom, throwing on a pair of jeans and a sweatshirt, covering every bit of skin from her ankles to her neck. When she returned to the door, she pushed down her embarrassment, threw back her shoulders and opened the door, calm, cool and collected.

The cable guy and his van had disappeared. In their place were a big black, four-wheel drive pickup truck and Colin McFarlan.

"Why couldn't you have been five lousy minutes earlier?" she wailed and waved him into the house.

"I was going to wait in my truck, but the cable guy took off, squealing tires. I was afraid something might be wrong."

Wrong was an understatement.

As she closed the door, Fancy's frustration, embarrassment and nerves bubbled up her throat and erupted into sidesplitting belly laughs that had her doubled over clutching her tummy.

Colin waited quietly until her laughter turned into giggles and faded away.

His brows wrinkled. "Do you mind telling me what's so funny?"

She shook her head. "Sorry. I can't."

"It's about eighty-five degrees outside. Are you wearing that to the fair?"

She glanced down at the sweatshirt, her lips twitching. "No. Give me a minute." Dashing for her bedroom, she slammed the door behind her as a way to keep herself from asking him to join her.

After nearly flashing the cable guy, her lusty

passion had deflated considerably. But with Colin in the other room…

Fancy quickly changed into dressy shorts, a cotton blouse she tied at the waist and strappy flat sandals. A quick brush through her hair and she was ready to leave.

When she stepped out of the bedroom, her heart leaped to her throat.

In her earlier rush to get to the door, she'd set BOB on the end table beside the couch.

Colin had taken a position in a chair opposite the couch and now stared from her to BOB and back, his brows dipped. "Do I want to know what happened with you and the cable guy?"

"No." She grabbed BOB and hid it behind her back. "Why don't you get a couple of beers out of the refrigerator while I…put this away?"

His frown deepened. "Are you and the cable guy…?"

Her brows shot up. "Oh, heavens no. I think I scared the poor guy to death." She chuckled. "I don't think he'll come back."

"Good." Colin's scowl lightened and he reached into the refrigerator, extracting two bottles of Miller Lite. "I would have thought you'd have switched from beer to fancy wine, with your life in Dallas."

Fancy shook her head. "Nothing is as good as a cold beer on a hot Texas day. I used to love drinking beer with you and your brothers after we hauled hay."

Colin twisted the top off one bottle and handed it to her. "I remember. You drove the truck."

"I offered to throw hay bales, but you McFarlans wouldn't hear of it."

"We were afraid you might break a nail."

She frowned. "I'm not all fluff, you know."

"And you could ride a horse like nobody's business back then. Do you still ride?"

She shook her head. "I haven't had the chance."

"We'll have to remedy that." He twisted the top off his beer and drank a long swallow. "Now, about the device you put away."

Her pulse quickened. "I'd rather not talk about it."

"I find the subject...interesting." Colin tipped his beer and drank.

"Sadly, it wasn't, and then it was just embarrassing." Her cheeks burned as she recalled the horrified expression on the cable guy's face. "Could we please not talk about it? And since you're here so early, maybe we can stop by the hardware store if it's still open and buy some batteries?"

In mid-swallow when Fancy dropped that last request on him, Colin spewed beer across the room and broke into a fit of coughing.

Other than having to clean up the beer, Fancy was proud of her comment. Let him stew on that a while.

Not that she wanted to be a tease, but he wouldn't let the subject drop.

She upended her beer, drank it down in several gulps and licked the drops from her lips. "Ready?"

Colin's gaze zeroed in on her lips. "More than you'll know."

Fancy's core heated and her pussy ached. *Holy hell.* The way he was looking at her like she was the main course and he was a starving animal...*oy!* If she didn't leave soon, she'd be dragging him into her bedroom and kicking BOB to the curb. She grabbed her purse and one of his hands. "Come on. Let's go to the fair." At least at the fair they'd be surrounded by people. Nothing sexy could happen with so many people around them.

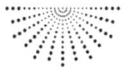

CHAPTER FIVE

*C*olin's thoughts kept straying to that silver dildo standing proudly on Fancy's end table. Walking from the parking area to the fairgrounds with his cock straining against his blue jeans made every step Colin took painful.

He'd arrived early at Fancy's house with the intention of seducing and making sweet love to her before they headed for the fairgrounds.

If they made it to the fair at all.

Her laughter had put the kibosh on his intention, taking the wind out of his sails. Until she'd run off to dress and he noticed the sex toy on her end table.

What sweet hell was this? She used toys to get off? He'd been so fascinated by the idea he'd stared at the toy until she appeared in the doorway looking all flushed and pretty in her shorts. Those long, bare legs stretched from her feet practically to her chin, and they'd been wrapped around his waist the night before.

Colin had wanted to march her back to her bedroom and take her then and there. He might even take the toy with them. The possibilities were positively titillating.

But when Fancy came out of the bedroom, she shut the door firmly behind her, making it clear that room was off limits.

She'd be a tough nut to crack, but crack her, he would.

Challenge accepted, sweetheart.

Mentally rolling up his sleeves, he concentrated on finding opportunities to get her alone, while stalking his mother and her date to keep them from being alone. It promised to be an interesting evening.

"We should hang out at the entrance and wait for my uncle and your mother," Fancy said.

"Or we can get cotton candy and throw a few rings over the soda pop bottles." Colin led her toward the carnival booths, scoping the larger rides and attractions for possibilities of alone time. The Ferris wheel and the Fun House were about the only places he could get Fancy alone. And if he slipped the carnie a fifty, he might stop the Ferris wheel at the top for long enough to...whatever she'd let him get away with.

Colin stopped in front of the booth with the guns shooting water into a ring.

A little boy gave the carnie a dollar and the man set him up on one of the guns.

Colin recognized the four-year-old. "Dalton, is that you?"

The boy smiled up at him. "Oh, hello, Uncle Colin."

Colin glanced around for the boy's mother.

Gwen stood nearby. "Hi, Colin. Angus didn't tell me you were going to be here."

"I didn't know I would either, until about an hour ago." He pulled Fancy against his side. "Fancy, this is Gwen, Angus's fiancée, and Dalton, here, is her son."

Fancy shook hands with Gwen. "Nice to meet you. Congratulations."

"Thank you."

The carnival worker cleared his throat. "Do you want to play, mister?"

"Since Dalton is playing, we should join him." Colin handed him money for all three of the adults.

They stood at the guns and the carnival worker told them to start.

Dalton, Gwen, Colin and Fancy pressed their triggers and water squirted out. Colin's stream hit dead center of his ring and filled the balloon behind it. Dalton, Gwen and Fancy only managed a little water in their balloons. At the end of the allotted time, Colin won the shooting match and the carnie gave him a choice of prizes. He glanced at Fancy. "Is there something you would like, or we could pass on our good fortune to someone else?" He tilted his head toward the Dalton.

The little boy sighed and stared up at the prizes he missed out on. His mother put her hand on his shoulder. "Come on, let's find another game."

Fancy followed Colin's lead. "I'll pass."

Colin swung Dalton up on his arm. "You forgot your prize."

"But I didn't win," Dalton said. "You did."

"And I want you to have it."

Dalton hugged Colin's neck. "Thank you, Uncle Colin." He stared at the prizes for a long moment and then pointed to a gaudy tiara with shiny pink and purple fake stones. "I want that."

Colin's brow puckered. "You sure you don't want the sling shot or the cowboy hat?"

Dalton shook his head. "No. I want the crown."

The carnie handed him the crown, Colin set Dalton on the ground, and the boy ran over to his mother. "This is for you."

Gwen bent to take the tiara from him. "Oh, sweetie, this is the most beautiful crown I've ever seen." She put it on her head and modeled it. "I love it."

Dalton hugged her and then pushed away.

Angus arrived carrying two sticks of cotton candy.

Dalton ran to Angus and hugged him around the

knees. Then he pointed at Gwen's head. "Mr. Angus, look what I got for Mommy."

Angus smiled at the crown. "I like it."

Colin's heart twinged at the happy little family in front of him. He could picture him and Fancy with a little Fancy or Colin eager to ride the rides at the fair. It struck him then, this was what he'd been missing. Not only did he want Fancy in his bed where he could make love to her for the rest of his life, but he wanted the entire package—Fancy, kids, a home together, baseball and soccer practice, ballet recitals —the whole nine yards.

For a moment he couldn't breathe past the incredible longing squeezing his chest. He turned to Fancy and held out his hand. "Ready for some of that cotton candy?" *And for you and me to start a family?*

He bit down hard on his tongue to keep from blurting out what he really wanted. The woman was dead set on keeping him at arm's length. He had to take it slow or risk her thinking he was insincere, only wanting to get into her panties and tossing her like last weeks' rotten tomatoes.

Fancy drew in a deep breath and looked up at him with a wide smile and suspiciously shiny eyes. "I'd love some cotton candy."

She slipped her hand into his. No argument.

Colin would count that as progress. If he played his cards right, he might convince her he wasn't the hit-and-run wreck every female in the county claimed.

FANCY SWALLOWED the lump lodged in her throat. Seeing Gwen, Angus and Dalton together had been a blow to her already aching heart, and the reason she'd come back to Temptation to exorcise Colin's memories so she could get on with her life.

Angus and his fiancée had what Fancy wanted— the perfect little family, love and a future together. They looked so stinking happy, like they belonged.

Her eyes blurring, Fancy let Colin lead her away from Angus and his family. They stopped in front of the stand where a woman spun sugar into cotton candy.

"Blue or pink?" Colin asked.

"Blue." It matched her mood.

"I'd have taken you for a pink kinda girl."

"It's sugar and food coloring. What does it matter?"

When he handed her the thin paper cone capped with a cloud of blue cotton candy, Fancy took it and tore off a sticky swath and shoved it into her mouth. The sugar dissolved on her tongue, sweet and gritty, reminding her of going to the fair with her parents when she was young. As an only child, her parents had showered her with everything, including cotton candy. They'd been a tight-knit family unit.

Colin opted for pink cotton candy, bringing a smile to Fancy's face.

"I would have taken you for a blue cotton candy guy."

"To me, cotton candy isn't right unless it's pink." He tore off a wad of the feathery concoction and stuffed it into his mouth, some of the pink dissolving on his lips.

Fancy swallow hard, fighting the urge to lick the candy off him. Instead, she focused on her blue cloud of sugar. Anything but Colin and his kissable face. "Doesn't pink damage your male ego?"

"Not at all." He glanced up. "There they are."

Fancy turned toward the fairgrounds entrance gate.

Uncle Carl entered with Maggie McFarlan on his arm. He was laughing at something she said. Every time Fancy saw them together, they appeared happy and always smiling at each other. It seemed a shame to break up a happy couple.

But Fancy didn't want to deal with the alternative. Staring across the room at Colin and his latest conquest would be difficult. Perhaps by that time, Fancy would be glad she hadn't fallen for him—glad she'd held out for a man who would love her forever, not just for a night or two.

Somehow the vision in her head didn't include a man for her. Only another woman for Colin.

"Ready?" Colin held out his arm.

Fancy opted to ignore his invitation and fell in step beside him without touching. She'd be better off weaning herself from Colin now.

"Colin, Fancy, we didn't expect to see you two here." Mrs. M smiled, though her smile appeared strained.

After the craziness of the previous night, Fancy didn't look forward to ruining their evening, but she'd promised to help Colin. And she had a stake in this as well. "Uncle Carl, Mrs. M. Just the folks we were hoping to run into."

Uncle Carl's brows pulled together. "You were?"

"Yes. We'd like to apologize for last night, wouldn't we?" Fancy elbowed Colin in the gut.

"Uh, yes." Colin rubbed his belly. "We would. I must have had too much to drink."

"A good thing Angus drove last night." Mrs. M nodded. "At least he had his head on his shoulders."

"Right. Colin was in no shape to drive," Fancy added. "We'd like to spend time with you both this evening to show you Colin can behave when he wants to."

"Oh, that's not necessary," Mrs. M assured them.

"But we insist." Colin cupped his mother's elbow and led her away from Uncle Carl.

Fancy hooked her arm through her uncle's and smiled up at him. "It will give us time to catch up. I haven't seen much of you over the past couple of weeks. How are the renovations coming along?"

Her uncle stared down at her. "Fine. But then you know that. You've been working with the contractor as much as I have."

"True. But I haven't been out there in a couple days and you probably have."

Colin and Mrs. M were a couple yards ahead of them when Uncle Carl leaned close to Fancy. "What are you two doing?"

She glanced up at her uncle, her brows rising. "I don't know what you're talking about. Is it a crime to want to spend time with my uncle? My only living relative?"

"Yes, when you're obviously trying to keep me from Maggie." Carl stopped and faced Fancy, his posture stiff, a frown settling on his forehead. "Colin, I understand. He and his brothers don't know me and certainly don't trust anyone with their sweet mama." He shook his head. "But you... Why?"

Rather than answer his question, she asked, "Why are you dating Maggie?"

Her uncle relaxed and a smile drifted across his face. "You might not think older people can fall in and out of love, but I've been in love with Maggie since before she married John McFarlan. As teens, the three of us were inseparable. Until John asked her to marry him the day we all graduated from high school."

"He beat you to her?" She started walking again and her uncle fell in step beside her.

"He did. And she said yes." Her uncle scrubbed a hand down his face. "I chose to step out of the picture. John was a good man—a better man than I was, and she was happy with him. They had three fine sons and a good life together."

"John died more than eight years ago. Why didn't you come back sooner?"

"You don't know how much I wanted to, but her sons were there for her and I didn't want her to think I was insincere, poaching on a dead man's widow."

"You never married," Fancy said, her heart tightening. "Because you were always in love with another man's wife?"

Uncle Carl patted her hand. "For me, I'm a one-woman man."

"Then why did they call you the Heartbreaker?"

He snorted. "I didn't say I was celibate. I just never let another woman close enough. Whenever a woman wanted more, I let her go. My heart always belonged to Maggie."

"Are you two coming?" Colin called out from ahead.

He and Mrs. M stood in front of the Fun House, tickets in hand.

"If you'll excuse me, my date is waiting." He disengaged his arm from Fancy's, grabbed Maggie's hand and hurried toward the entrance to the Fun House.

Colin held up two tickets. "What was keeping you two?"

"We were talking." Fancy took the tickets from Colin's hand and handed them to the carnival worker. "Come on. We need to keep up with them." She didn't want to go into the details of what her uncle told her. The way it stood, her heart wasn't into coming between her uncle and his only love. Knowing what she did made it seem mean and spiteful to keep the two apart.

Colin handed her into the big Fun House trailer and turned to say a few words to the carnival worker before he entered. They stepped into a glass and mirrored maze, stretching the length of the trailer.

The giggles of others who'd gone ahead echoed back to them.

Fancy walked to what she thought was the opening only to find it was a trick of the mirrors and was a dead end. "How do we get through?"

Colin grinned. "This way." He led her through an opening to the next passage where their reflections were distorted. One mirror made Fancy's head appear to be as big as a medicine ball, the next made her look short and fat. The next mirror made her look like a giant Q-tip, her middle pencil thin, her head and feet huge.

She glanced at Colin in front of the short and fat mirror and she burst out laughing.

He grabbed her hand and pulled her against his side. "Now we both look the same."

"This is what eating too much cotton candy will

do to us." She laughed again. Seeing Colin short tickled her funny bone.

Colin turned to her and cupped her face with one of his hands, smoothing his thumb across her cheek. "You should laugh more."

She stared up at him in the dim lighting, her gaze captured by the intensity of his dark eyes. More than anything, she wanted to kiss him. But she'd followed her misguided instincts more than once with Colin and it led to heartache. "We should catch up with the others."

"We will," he said, stepping closer, his other hand curving around her waist to press against her back. "In a moment."

Being alone with Colin was a very bad thing. It made her forget what she was trying so hard to do.

He tipped her head up and bent down until his mouth was a mere inch from hers.

"What are you doing?" she asked, her voice a whisper in the suddenly silent trailer.

"I would think you'd know by now."

"I don't want to kiss you," she lied.

"Then don't." His breath was warm and minty against her lips a tempting promise of a kiss.

Fancy wanted it, but refused to rise up and take it. "You're the devil."

"I've been called that before," he said, still refusing to go the extra inch to claim her mouth, daring her.

All she had to do was rise up on her toes. One lousy inch. Her feet flexed and she rose.

"Damn you," she said as her lips connected with his. Electricity shot through her body, zinging from nerve to nerve, coiling at her core in a flash of heat so intense it made her breath catch and hold.

Her fingers climbed up his chest and linked behind his head, drawing him closer, deepening the kiss.

He held back, letting her sweep past his lips to engage his tongue in a sensuous dance.

When she slid her leg along the back of his, his hands found her hips and pulled her close, the ridge of his cock encased in thick blue jeans nudged her belly, making her wish she'd invited him into her bedroom. The Fun House was no place to be when the desire to make love swept over her in an overwhelmingly hot surge that threatened to destroy all her plans to rid her body and mind of the one man who had never left her thoughts in the past eight years.

Sanity reared its persistent head and created a crevice in her wicked desire. It was small but grew. Finally, Fancy pushed away from Colin, stepping back.

His arms fell to his sides, his chest rising and falling like a runner at the end of a race.

"We should go before..." Fancy wiped the back of her hand over her kiss-swollen lips.

Colin reached out. "Before we make love again?"

She shook her head and took another step backward, bumping against one of the mirrors. "Before we do something we'll regret."

"Trust me. I won't regret it."

"You might not, but I will." She closed her eyes and drew in a deep, cleansing breath and let it out. "I'm here for my uncle and your mother, not to start something that will only end in a mess."

"Who said it has to end in a mess?" Colin took another step toward her.

"I'm not young and naive anymore. I'm not going to fall into your arms and lose my head again." Fancy glanced around, desperately seeking the way out. "How do we get the hell out of here?" She hurried toward what she thought was the exit and bumped her nose into a mirror. Turning, she tried the next wall, her hands leading the way to spare her face another collision.

"Darlin', as much as I like watching your freak out over the maze, if you'll follow me, I'll get you out."

Disgruntled that she couldn't get herself out, she followed Colin, staying far enough behind that she didn't have to touch him, but close enough she didn't lose him. After what seemed a very long time, but could only have been five minutes or less, they emerged from the Fun House and descended the steps to the ground.

Fancy glanced around, desperate to find Maggie

and Uncle Carl. Her plan wouldn't work if she allowed herself to be alone with Colin. Her resistance was crumbling and she was quickly losing the will to fight. She had to get away, restore her senses and get her shit together.

"Colin! Oh my God! Is that you?"

Fancy skidded to a halt and turned to see a gorgeous redhead drape her arms around Colin's neck and planted her lips on his in a loud, wet kiss.

His lips had moments before been on hers and, from where Fancy was standing, Colin didn't appear to mind.

Anger replaced helpless desperation. Fine. Let the poor deluded soul have him. What the women said about Colin McFarlan was true. He was a player, a hit-and-run heartbreaker. God, Fancy was glad his true colors came through before she'd fallen completely under his stupid spell.

She spun, tears welling in her eyes, and ran.

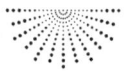

CHAPTER SIX

*C*olin unwrapped the woman's arms from around his neck and pushed her to arms' length, looking past her to Fancy's face, blanched of color. "Kylie, I'm busy. Do you mind?"

Kylie pouted and slipped her arms around his middle. "Oh, come on. Surely you can spare a minute or two to catch up with an old friend."

Fancy spun and ran the other direction.

"No, Kylie. I can't spare a second." He tried to step around Kylie.

Kylie was faster, moving to block his path with her body. "Not even for old time's sake?" She ran her fingers down the front of his shirt. "We were so good in bed. Can't we pick up where we left off?"

Not really. The woman was too noisy and raked him with her claws. And not in a good way. He didn't want to do it, but some women required the blunt truth.

"Kylie, I have no intention of picking up where we left off. I'm not interested. I love someone else." He gripped her arms, moved her to the side and ran after Fancy.

"You could have been a little more sensitive, Colin," Kylie yelled after him. "Damn cowboys."

Colin didn't look back, his gaze panning the crowd, searching for Fancy. She couldn't be that far ahead. He spotted her next to a merry-go-round, talking to her uncle and Colin's mother.

"Oh, there's Colin now. He's not lost at all." His mother smiled and waved toward him. "Colin, honey, Fancy's ready to leave. Carl would have taken her, if we couldn't find you, but now that you're here…"

Colin captured Fancy's elbow in his hand. "Thank you, Mom. I'll handle this."

"Good." His mother turned to Carl. "Let's go."

As soon as the older couple stepped away, Fancy jerked her arm out of Colin's grip. "You don't have to leave on my account. I'll find alternate transportation."

"If you want to go home, I'll take you. Just give me a minute to explain."

She snorted. "Explain what? You're entitled to whatever or whoever you want to do. I'm not your keeper."

Gripping her arm again, he led her toward the

Ferris wheel and handed over two tickets. "Get in the seat."

She stood with her feet braced and her arms crossed over her chest. "I'm not going on the Ferris wheel with you."

"I would like the opportunity to talk. Uninterrupted."

Fancy shook her head. "No."

"We'll just talk."

"No."

He lifted her hand and threaded his fingers with hers. "Please."

Fancy rolled her eyes and sighed. "I'm going to regret this," she muttered. "Fine. I'll ride the damned Ferris wheel with you, but it won't change my mind."

Colin handed Fancy into the seat and turned to the operator, slipping him a fifty dollar bill. Beneath his breath he said, "I like the view from the top, if you get my drift."

The man winked and waited until Colin settled in the seat beside Fancy. Then he flipped a lever and set the Ferris wheel in motion and it rose to the top, around and back to the bottom, settling into a slow rhythm of revolutions.

"I'm here. Talk," Fancy said, staring straight ahead.

"I haven't gone out with Kylie in over a year. She wasn't right for me and I told her that. It turns out she's hard to convince."

At the top again, the Ferris wheel jerked and

groaned.

Fancy reached for his hand. "What was that?"

Not above taking advantage of her when she was frightened, Colin scooted closer to her and tightened his fingers around hers. "It's an old machine. They make noises. Probably needs a little oil."

"Okay. So why are you telling me about Kylie? Like I said, you have a right to be with whomever you want. I'm not stopping you."

"I'm telling you because the women I've been with before never worked out."

"Including me," she said, her tone flat.

"That wasn't because we weren't compatible. What happened between you and me was a timing issue. The other women weren't right because they weren't you."

There. He'd said it, opened his mouth and heart. He lifted her hand and pressed a kiss to the backs of her knuckles.

She didn't pull away. That was a good sign. If she really didn't want him to kiss her, she would have yanked her hand—

Fancy jerked her hand from his. "Colin, I came back to Temptation to purge you from my life, not reunite."

His stomach lurched, from the ragged stop and start of the Ferris wheel and from her words. "You came to what?"

"To get you out of my system. I need to move on

with my life."

Hurt and a little angry, he asked, "How's that working for you?"

She snorted. "Not so good."

His lips quirked into a smile. "You mean making love in the storeroom wasn't part of the plan?"

She shook her head and chuckled, the sound catching at the end. "Hell no."

"And kissing me in the Fun House wasn't furthering your goals." He turned in his seat and cupped her face in his palm. "And kissing me now would shoot your plans all to hell."

"Yes," she whispered, her gaze slipping to his mouth, her tongue darting out to swipe across her lips. "All to hell. Ah, hell." She reached out, captured the back of his head and drew him close, claiming his mouth, twisting her tongue around his.

At that exact moment, the Ferris wheel jerked to a halt, rocking the seat.

Fancy broke away. "We're stopped."

"Maybe they're letting someone else off."

"Oh." She smiled and captured his face in her hands. "Where were we? Oh, right. I was making a big mistake." Again, she kissed him, long and deep, scooting closer on the seat until she was almost draped across his lap.

Colin's arms wrapped around her, crushing her to him. For once in his life, he was afraid. Afraid if he let go, he'd lose her forever. Eight years fell away and he felt what he'd felt all that time ago. A deep connection that refused to be ignored.

She ran her hand across his chest, slipping fingers inside his shirt, her soft skin against his making him crazy.

Colin slipped his hand beneath the tied-off edge of her shirt, running it up her torso to cup a full, luscious breast in his palm. He toyed with the nipple through the lace cup, tapping, flicking and pinching it, fabric and all.

Fancy caught his hand and pulled it away from her breast and angled downward to the waistband of her shorts.

With no idea how long they'd be stalled, Colin went with the invitation and slid his fingers into the waistband of her shorts and cupped the triangle of material over her sex.

Moaning, Fancy covered his hand and pressed it hard against her, curling her fingers around his, urging him to take more. Then she unbuttoned and unzipped her shorts, allowing him more room to maneuver.

Heart pounding, adrenaline shooting through him, Colin pushed aside the silky panties, slipped between her folds and stroked the strip of flesh hidden there.

"Oh my," she said, her voice catching, her hips rising to him. "Again."

He smiled and complied, first dipping his finger

in the cream of her pussy and then dragging the moisture up to her clit. Then he laid siege to her, flicking, stroking, swirling and pinching that most sensitive area on her body. He dipped into her again, thrusting one, then two, then three fingers into her drenched channel.

Her pussy clenched, sucking his fingers deeper. He pumped in and out of her. His fingers wet with her juices, he slipped them back in her folds and took her to the edge.

She clung to him, her hand covering his, alternating pulling his fingers away and pressing them deeper. Then her hips rocked into him, her back arching against the seat, and she sucked in a sharp breath.

Colin's cock, hard as steel, pushed against the placard of his jeans, straining to get out and thrust into her warm wet channel. There just wasn't a way to manage it on a Ferris wheel and be safe, or he'd have done it.

Her body rigid, her eyes squeezed tightly shut and her pussy creaming around his fingers, Fancy was the most beautiful woman Colin had ever been with. The passion of her release shook her body.

The Ferris wheel lurched and their seat at the top dropped an inch, stopped and then continued its slow descent, stopping for each car to offload passengers.

Colin pulled his hands from her shorts and wiped

her juices off on the leg of his jeans, satisfied she'd come with such complete abandon.

Fancy scrambled to button and zip her shorts and retie her shirt before their seat reached the bottom.

The operator opened the gate and let them off, winking at Colin as he passed.

If he thought the site of the dildo had him horny, watching Fancy come at the top of the Ferris wheel had Colin so wound up he wasn't sure he could make it back to his truck without hurting himself.

He prayed that wasn't the end of the evening with Fancy.

FANCY STAGGERED down the stairs from the Ferris wheel, her knees shaking, her entire world spinning. Not from the ride, but from what happened at the top.

"Where are my uncle and your mother? We should find them," she said half-heartedly, surprised she could sound so calm when electrical currents rippled around her insides, the residual effect of a giant orgasm in a public place.

"I don't know." Colin stopped in the middle of main walkway and carefully adjusted his jeans, without being too obvious about it.

A smile curled Fancy's lips at the size of the bulge beneath his zipper. He had to be in physical pain, the denim stretched tight over his package.

Her breathing grew more ragged. "I think they left. You might as well take me home."

"Good." He grabbed her hand and walked somewhat bowlegged toward the exit, steady but gingerly.

Once in the cab of the truck, Fancy chewed on her lower lip. Her plan was falling apart around her. After the incredible release, she rode a post-coital high, her body flushed with residual heat, her insides humming with continued desire.

When Colin pulled into her driveway, she waited for him to come around to open her door for her, knowing he would wrap his hands around her waist to help her out.

When he did, she slid down his front, the hard ridge of his erection searing a path across her sex and belly until her feet touched the ground. She entwined her arms around his neck and gave in to the longing. "Wanna finish what you started?"

He closed his eyes and drew in a long, steadying breath and let it out slowly. "I thought you'd never ask." Then he swung her up in his arms and strode for her front door.

Fancy dug in her purse for her key, slid it in the lock and turned. The door opened. "You can put me down now."

"Uh-uh." Colin didn't set her on her feet until he'd carried her across the threshold and kicked the door closed behind them. He lowered her legs, holding her body close to him, and then bent to capture her lips with his in a deep, breath-stealing kiss.

Fancy leaned into him, her fingers bunching his shirt, her insides heating again, ready to take him as soon as they both were naked.

When he let her up for air, she laughed shakily. "I could have walked in on my own feet."

"I liked my way better."

"Were you afraid I'd get away?"

He brushed a strand of her hair behind her ear. "Yes."

She slipped her hands behind his neck and dragged his mouth down to hers. "That wasn't even a possibility after that incredible Ferris wheel ride." Fancy took the lead on the kiss this time, tracing the seam of his lips until he opened to her. She toyed with his tongue and ended the kiss by capturing his bottom lip between her teeth, tugging gently.

Moving down his neck, she kissed a path to the top button of his shirt. One by one she flicked the buttons loose with her fingers until she reached his belt buckle. She pulled the shirt out of his jeans and finished the job.

"Woman…" Colin growled and brushed aside her hands.

"What?"

"You take too long." He yanked the shirt from his shoulders and tossed it to the corner.

"Don't believe much in foreplay?" She untied her

shirt, taking her sweet time.

"What are you talking about? This whole evening has been nothing but foreplay from the moment I sat on your couch earlier to now."

"You're a little fixated on BOB, aren't you?" She eased the buttons loose on her shirt until the last one.

"Seriously?" He reached out and pushed the last one through. "You called me a heartbreaker. But you're a tease."

"Getting to you?" Fancy turned away and slid the shirt halfway down her back.

"Enough." He lunged for her, snagging the collar of her blouse.

Fancy squealed and leaped forward, letting him have the shirt. She raced for the bedroom, grabbing her purse with the batteries they'd purchased at the hardware store on their way to the fair earlier.

As she ran, she kicked off her shoes, unbuttoned her shorts, shoved them over her hips and nearly tripped stepping out of them. The bra came next and the panties last. When she came to a stop by the bed, she turned to find Colin naked and advancing toward her.

Fancy reached into the nightstand and pulled out the shiny dildo and placed it into his hand.

His gaze skimmed down her body, over her breasts and lower, his nostrils flaring. He held out his other hand. "Batteries?"

Fancy fumbled in her purse for the package,

pulled it out and slapped it into Colin's hand. While he replaced the batteries in BOB, she studied his body, admiring the breadth of his shoulders, the way his muscles rippled when he moved, the tight, washboard abs and narrow waist. Oh, and those tight, muscular thighs…

The man was beautiful. And that didn't even begin to describe his hard, thick staff, jutting straight out, getting larger the more she watched.

He snapped the end shut on the toy and flipped the switch. It vibrated with vigor. Between the buzz of the sex toy and the real thing standing at attention, Fancy's pussy creamed.

"Enough," she echoed his earlier statement, grabbed his hand and dragged him toward the bed. "I like to finish what I've started." She crawled up on the mattress and lay back against the pillows.

"I like the way you think." He dropped down beside her, BOB in hand.

Her insides tingled in anticipation of both Colin and BOB making love to her at the same time. The night was getting better by the minute.

Colin leaned over and kissed her. What started as a light brush of his lips, progressed into a deep, sensuous joining of their mouths.

When Fancy tried to slide her leg up over his, his hand blocked her. He gently laid her leg on the bed, spreading her wide, exposing her wet pussy to the cool air.

With nothing cool in his dark eyes, he stared down at her, his gaze taking her in from her lips downward. His glance skimmed over her breasts and his nostrils flared. He didn't touch, but continued his perusal all the way to the apex of her thighs where her clit throbbed, her core burned and her pussy drenched, ready for him.

Just when she thought she might explode with expectant desire, he laid cool, hard BOB on her belly. The vibrations resonated throughout her body.

Slowly, he moved the device up to her left breast, curling it around the full circumference.

The combination of the toy and his hungry gaze ignited a fire inside Fancy and her back arched off the bed.

A smile curled the corners of Colin's lips and he bent to take the opposite nipple into his mouth. He sucked gently, then rolled the hardened bead on his tongue, nipping softly.

Fancy moaned, her hand sliding down her side to the tuft of hair over her sex. She slid a finger between her folds and flicked her clit, her breath catching at her body's immediate response.

Colin chuckled. "Am I not moving fast enough?"

"Oh, you're doing great," Fancy said, her voice breathy, her lungs unable to bring in the air she needed to survive. Her other hand skimmed across his naked back, sliding low to cup his tight ass in her palm. *Sweet pickles!* He was hard all over.

Sucking the other nipple into his mouth, Colin drew hard on it, laving it with his tongue until the tip puckered into a tight little nub.

Then he shifted his weight, moving down her body, BOB leading, his lips and tongue following, touching every inch, every rib. When he reached her triangle of curls, he slid BOB in first, parting her folds with his fingers. Cool air wafted over her heated clit.

Colin touched that strip of flesh with the vibrator, sending tingles across the sensitive nerves.

Fancy laced her fingers into his hair and moaned. "Wow. It never felt that good before."

"Baby, just wait." He slid BOB down to her entrance and eased it in her drenched channel, the steady vibrations making her body hum. "Now this." He bent to flick her clit with his tongue.

The combination of his warm, wet tongue, the shimmy of the sex toy inside and having Colin in her bed was more than Fancy could have imagined. "Oh, sweet heaven!"

Colin chuckled, the warmth of his breath brushing across her mons. He tongued her again, shifting the vibrator as he did.

Fancy gasped, drew her knees up and dug her heels into the mattress. "More!"

Swirling his tongue and the vibrator, he laid siege to her, conquering her in flicks and nibbles until she rocketed over the edge, her body straining to milk every last sensation out of the most incredible orgasm she'd ever experienced.

As she fell back to earth, she gripped Colin's ears and pulled.

"Hey! Go easy." He laughed, crawling up her body, sneaking a nibble of her breast before he settled his big frame between her legs. His cock nudged her entrance. "Damn. We need protection."

"In the nightstand," she said through gritted teeth. If she didn't have him inside her soon, she'd fall completely to pieces.

He leaned across her, reaching into the drawer where he found an accordion of condoms. Holding them up, he cocked a brow. "Expecting someone?"

"Prince Charming. Hurry, damn it." Her pussy throbbed, her pulse hammered and she couldn't remember ever being this impatient to have a man inside her.

Quickly applying the rubber, he was back in place, his shaft poised for entry. "First, a kiss."

"Yes," she said, her fingers curling around his gorgeous ass. She leaned up to accept his lips. At the same time, she gripped his buttocks and slammed him home.

He slid in, stretching her channel, filling her so full she could barely breathe. When his balls bumped into her bottom, she had him all. This was where she'd always wanted to be—in Colin's arms, with him inside her. There was no other place better.

He settled into a hard and fast rhythm, pumping in and out of her, increasing the speed and intensity.

She lifted her hips, meeting him with each thrust until she burst up over the top again, her fingers dug into his hips and she held on until he slammed into her one more time.

His body tensed and his cock pulsed inside her. For a long moment he held himself buried deep within her until his body went limp. Colin dropped to the bed beside her, rolling her to face him without losing their intimate connection.

"That was amazing," he whispered into her ear.

"Amazing." Fancy trailed her fingers across his massive chest, loving the feeling of him inside her still.

Being with Colin like this blew her original plans all to hell. How could she get him out of her system when all she wanted was to be with him forever?

Deep in her heart, she imagined a future with Colin. Could he be committed to her for the rest of their lives together? Or would he tire of her and leave her for another woman?

At that moment, she was willing to take her chances. She couldn't conceive of loving any other man. Colin was the one she wanted.

She'd be opening her heart for potential heartbreak.

So be it.

CHAPTER SEVEN

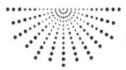

*C*olin woke to the tantalizing scent of bacon cooking. Had Jessie mastered the art of frying bacon without burning it? He opened his eyes and took a moment to focus on the unfamiliar surroundings. Then he remembered. He'd spent the night with Fancy in her house, making love to her into the early hours of the morning.

The bed beside him was empty, but her scent lingered in the sheets and pillows.

Inhaling deeply, Colin rose and stepped into the adjoining bathroom. After a quick shower, he toweled dry and slipped into his jeans. He tucked one of the spare foil packages into his back pocket and then he went in search of the woman and the bacon, knowing what he wanted first.

Fancy stood at the stove in the kitchen, barefoot, her blond hair pulled back from her face in a ponytail, and she wore his shirt with the sleeves rolled up to her elbows. And she appeared to be wearing nothing else.

Holy hell.

He reached for her and pulled her back against him. "Something smells good."

"Bacon and scrambled eggs."

"I wasn't talking about the food." He slipped his hands beneath the shirt. No panties. He ran his hands down to her mound and played with the curls there.

She pressed her bottom into his bulge. "I'm going to burn the bacon."

"Turn it off."

Fancy reached for the control on the stove and switched off the burner. Then she relaxed against him, lifting her arms over her head to wrap her hands around his neck.

Colin swept his hands up her sides and cupped her breasts, weighing them in his palms. Then he pinched the nipples, nuzzling her neck at the same time.

"I might enjoy cooking more if I did it like this every time," she said.

"The kitchen is highly underrated." He nipped the back of her ear and splayed his hands over her belly, angling lower to the juncture of her thighs. Colin's cock hardened as his fingers threaded through the springy curls over her sex and parted her folds.

"Oh, yes." Fancy ran her hands over his hips and

cupped his ass, her head leaning back, resting on his chest.

He stroked her nubbin, dipped his finger into her pussy and stroked again and again.

When her body tensed and her hands gripped his buttocks, he stopped, spun her around and lifted her, setting her on the table.

She jerked his button free and eased his zipper down.

His cock sprang free into her capable palm. She guided it to her entrance, spreading her knees wide. Then her hands moved to his hips.

"Wait." Colin reached into his back pocket and held out the prize.

Fancy grabbed it from him, tore open the foil and rolled the condom down over his staff.

Needing no further encouragement, he plunged into her, her wet pussy making it a smooth, tight glide home.

With her hands guiding him, Colin thrust again and again. The table screeched across the floor and dishes rattled. When he climaxed, he felt Fancy's body tense at the same time. They rode the wave together until they drifted into shore, sexually replete.

Colin pressed a kiss to her damp forehead and slid out.

"And I'm supposed to function after that?" Fancy

drew in a breath and let it out. When she scooted off the table, her knees buckled.

Reaching out, Colin steadied her, pulling her into his arms. Her body fit his perfectly, every curve melding with his harder planes. He wanted this woman in his life forever. He kissed the top of her head and swatted her bottom. "Go get dressed while I finish cooking."

"Now, that's what I like to hear. A man who is confident in the kitchen."

"I don't know about that. After Jessie's numerous failures in the kitchen, I've had to figure out a few things. I think I can manage eggs and bacon."

"Then I'll grab a quick shower." Fancy stood on her tiptoes and kissed his lips, lingering to taste his tongue. "Umm. Better than bacon."

Colin chuckled, his gaze following her as she left the kitchen.

Smiling, he switched the stove on and finished frying the bacon, then scrambled eggs in a bowl and poured them into the pan.

A buzz sounded behind him and he turned to find Fancy's cell phone skittering across the table on vibrate.

Colin caught it before it fell to the floor.

The screen lit with a text message. If he hadn't saved the phone from falling, he wouldn't have seen who the text message was from.

Maggie McFarlan.

Colin frowned, his gaze scanning the message, a twinge of guilt burning in his chest for snooping into Fancy's business.

Why was his mother texting her? An image of them sitting at the table in the diner came to him. His mother had shoved papers into her purse to keep him from seeing them.

His mother's message read: *Still on for lunch to go over plans?*

Plans? What plans were his mother and Fancy cooking up? Then it hit him.

Fancy was a realtor.

Was his mother going ahead with her plan to sell the ranch? His hand tightened around the cell phone. In the back of his mind, he'd been positive his mother wouldn't go through with her threat to sell the ranch if he and his brothers didn't come up with fiancées or wives in the two months she gave them.

His heart dropped to his stomach. He'd be all right. He owned his own construction company and could find land and build his own house. But Angus had all his horses. Finding a place large enough would be time consuming and expensive. And he had a fiancée with a child to consider.

Then there was Brody who'd made an art studio out of the old hunting cabin in the middle of the ranch. He'd have to find a place big enough for a studio.

Not that they couldn't adjust, but...it was the

Rafter M. M for McFarlan. The ranch had been in the family for one hundred fifty years. All that history. The generations of McFarlans. All that would be lost. Some corporation would purchase the acreage and make it something depressing, a part of a conglomeration or something.

"Is breakfast ready?" Fancy's voice came to him from her bedroom.

Colin dropped the cell phone on the table as if it had scalded his hand.

Fancy knew what his mother was up to, but she hadn't bothered to tell him. Keeping a secret as big as that was almost as bad as betrayal.

After the crazy, wonderful night and morning they'd just spent together, Colin didn't know how to feel. One thing was for sure. He didn't feel like eating.

He scraped the scrambled eggs onto a plate, put the bacon next to it and set the table for one.

"Yum." Fancy entered the kitchen dressed in a baby-blue sundress that came down to mid-thigh. Her blond hair lay damp against her head, the ends curling as they dried.

Damn she was so fresh-faced and beautiful, it hurt to look at her.

When she looked into his eyes, her brows furrowed. "What's wrong?"

"I got a call from one of my job sites. I have to go," he lied.

"On Sunday?"

He shrugged. "It's behind schedule and the workers are putting in overtime to try to finish on time." Colin waved at the table. "You should eat while it's hot. I'll get dressed and show myself to the door."

"Are you sure it can't wait until after breakfast?"

"No. They had a hiccup and need my advice. I want to make sure they don't mess it up to delay even longer." He pressed a kiss to her forehead.

Her frown deepening, she gripped his arms. "Will I see you later?"

"I'll call," he said, forced a smile and then left her standing in the kitchen.

Colin hurried through the house to the bedroom where he gathered his clothing, dressed and slipped into his shoes. He needed to know the truth and he couldn't confront Fancy and confess he'd been reading her private text messages. He'd ask his mother. The sooner the better.

As he headed for the front door, Fancy stepped in front of him.

"Is this it? Is this the part where you dump the girl you're seeing?" She crossed her arms. "If so, tell me now so I don't spend the rest of the day waiting for your call."

"No, no. It's nothing like that. I really have to get to the job site." He bent and kissed her hard on the lips. "We'll talk later."

FANCY STARED at the door that closed behind Colin. What had just happened? One minute they're making love on the kitchen table, the next he was running out the door like a scalded cat.

She turned back to the kitchen, scraped the scrambled eggs and bacon into the trash, rinsed her plate and the pan and put them in the dishwasher. Her hunger of a few minutes ago had completely deserted her. She moved about the kitchen, forcing herself to continue to breathe and keep moving.

Maybe Colin was telling the truth. Maybe he really did have an emergency on the job site. That would explain why he looked like he had a lot on his mind. How could he switch from the loving, sexy man to the preoccupied one so quickly? Fancy couldn't. Ever since they'd rocked the kitchen table, she'd been walking around in a sex-induced haze.

Until Colin walked out the door.

With the kitchen clean, she had no reason to linger. Since it was Sunday, she didn't have any house or land showings that morning. Maybe a drive in the country would help clear her mind and settle her twisted stomach. By lunch she'd be okay for her meeting with Mrs. M. If she got up the courage, she'd ask the McFarlan matriarch what the hell was wrong with her son.

What worried her were all the warnings she'd received from her old friends. Colin was a player. Mr. Hit-and-Run. Love 'em and leave 'em was his motto. They'd warned her and Fancy had chosen to ignore them. Just like she'd ignored her plan for flushing him from her system. Her heart overruled her head, telling her she was different. He would fall in love with her and stay with her forever.

If Colin truly had hit and run, she had no one to blame but herself.

What a fool she'd been.

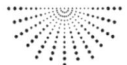

CHAPTER EIGHT

"*A*ngus! Brody! Mom!" Colin yelled as he stomped through the house. Where was everyone?

The kitchen was empty, dishes were put away and the smell of bacon lingered in the air.

A note on the refrigerator explained. *Gone to church.*

They wouldn't be back until after noon, which meant Colin wouldn't have any answers until then. With too much pent up energy, too many unanswered questions, Colin couldn't sit around and twiddle his thumbs.

He changed into work clothes and hit the barn where he mucked every stall, fed and watered the animals and still had an hour and a half until noon.

Saddling his buckskin gelding, he rode out across the pastures, hoping the wind in his hair would blow the concerns and feelings of betrayal out of his head. He'd thought what had happened between him and Fancy last night had changed everything.

He'd even begun to think she might come around to believing in a future with him. Then wham! That text message, his mother's threat coming true and him hopelessly in love with the woman who'd keep something like losing the family ranch from him.

No matter how hard he rode, the words on that text circled around and around in his mind. The implication settling heavy in his heart. He turned the horse around and headed back to the ranch. Maybe his mother had some documents in the house that would clear up the confusion.

Back at the barn, he quickly stowed the saddle, blanket and bridle and brushed the horse. He settled the gelding in his stall, gave him an extra bucket of feed and then headed to the house and into the ranch office. He searched through drawers, file cabinets and boxes and found nothing that indicated any sale of property. But he did find an envelope from a local attorney. The seal had been broken, so he pulled the letter out and read.

THANK you for your inquiry into the legal transfer of property. We would be happy to assist you in your endeavors. For a personal consultation, please schedule a meeting at your earliest convenience.

COLIN'S HEAD spun and his stomach clenched. Legal transfer? Holy hell, what was his mother doing? And how was Fancy helping? Was Carl Landers behind all of this? Had he convinced their mother to sell so he could get his hands on the cash? Colin didn't want to believe Fancy could be involved in a scam like that. But the man was her uncle.

He showered and changed into clean clothes and checked the clock. Twenty minutes until noon. Exactly the amount of time it took to get from the ranch to the diner in Temptation. He'd confront his mother and Fancy at the same time. Nothing like killing two birds with one stone. His only regret was that it would be in public.

"CHURCH GOT OUT EARLY, TODAY." Mrs. M smiled at Fancy. "Thank you for coming earlier."

"You're welcome. I'm glad I can help with the plans." Fancy stared down at the designs and samples she'd brought with her, her heart not at all into the conversation. But Mrs. M had insisted on helping and she was doing it as a favor to her Uncle Carl.

When Mrs. M offered to assist, Fancy was glad to let the older woman dig in and come up with the best alternatives to satisfy her uncle.

After Colin's hasty departure that morning, Fancy

couldn't concentrate on anything. Nothing made sense, especially one moody McFarlan who'd seemed to be as infatuated with her as she'd been with him last night and early this morning. She'd gone over and over everything that had happened and couldn't identify anything she could have done that he might have misconstrued.

Mrs. M reached across the table at PJ's Diner and laid her hand over Fancy's. "What's wrong, dear? You look sad."

For a long moment, Fancy stared at the older woman's hand on hers. She was like the mother Fancy had lost too early in life. And she really needed someone to talk to. But she was Colin's mother.

She sighed for the hundredth time. "Why would a man shower you with attention one minute and run away from you the next?"

"Sometimes men show you what you want to see until they get what they want. Then their real nature comes out." Mrs. M's brows puckered. "You were with Colin last night at the fair." Her eyes widened and she bit her lip. "Has my son said or done anything to hurt your feelings?"

Fancy shook her head and looked away as her eyes filled with tears she'd been holding back all morning. "I thought we had something going." She sniffed. "Then he left. No, he practically ran out the door." She raised her hands and stared across at the older woman through the tears. "What's wrong with me?"

"Honey, there's nothing wrong with you. You're beautiful inside and out. The question is what's wrong with that thickheaded son of mine?"

"Oh, Mrs. M, don't tell him I said anything. Please." Fancy dabbed at the tears on her cheeks. "Rejection is bad enough without the embarrassment of asking why."

"Are you sure he rejected you?"

"One minute he was totally into me. The next he was running out the door, claiming he had an emergency on a job site."

"He's been known to have emergencies on a job site."

"I know where his job sites are. I drove by. Nobody is working today." Her bottom lip trembled and she bit it to make it stop.

"I'm sorry, sweetie. I don't know what's gotten into his head. Maybe he got cold feet at the last minute. I've been pressuring the boys lately to get on with their lives. This could all be my fault."

Fancy gave Mrs. M a weak smile and patted her hand. "You didn't make him lie."

The older woman frowned. "I taught him better than that."

"Exactly." Fancy sat up straighter, brushing the moisture from her cheeks. "And I'll just have to get over it."

"Sorry I'm late." Uncle Carl slipped into the booth beside Maggie and kissed her cheek. "How are my two favorite girls?"

Maggie blushed. "I haven't been a girl for over forty years."

"You'll always be the prettiest girl in the state of Texas to me." He lifted her hand to his lips and kissed her knuckles. "When are you going to marry me and make me the happiest man alive?"

Both "girls" gasped.

"Carl, is that your idea of a proposal?"

"Well, it kind of slipped out. I've been waiting for the right time, but the right time seems to be now. I've waited for over thirty years, please tell me you won't make me wait longer."

Maggie opened her mouth to respond when another voice interrupted.

"Mom, what the hell's going on?"

Fancy turned to find Colin striding across the floor to stand at the end of their table.

Mrs. M frowned at her son. "Colin, that was rude to interrupt."

"I want to know what's going on. I believe I have every right to know."

His mother glared at him. "Until you approach me in a reasonable tone of voice with a reference to what you're talking about, I have nothing to say."

"Colin, perhaps you could wait until your mother

is home to question her," Uncle Carl suggested calmly.

COLIN GRABBED Carl by the front of his shirt and yanked him to his feet. "If you had kept out of our business and lives, none of this would be happening."

"Colin McFarlan, let go of Carl," his mother said. "If you're talking about the ultimatum, that's all my doing and I'm done talking about it."

Colin released Carl and planted his hands on the table. "I know what you're doing, Mom. And I know why you and Fancy have been meeting secretly."

"We haven't been meeting secretly. We've had lunch a few times here at the diner. Since when do you care what I do in my spare time?"

"Since you've contacted a lawyer and realtor to sell the Rafter M."

"What?" Three voices said the same word at once.

Colin stared from his mother to Carl, his gaze finally landing on Fancy. "You aren't helping Mom list the ranch?"

She crossed her arms, her brows drawn together. "No, I most certainly am not."

He turned to his mother, her face stormy. "And you're not getting with a lawyer to sell the ranch?"

"I'm getting with a lawyer, but not to sell the ranch."

Colin faced Carl, frowning. "Are you dating my

mother to get your hands on the ranch? Because, if you break her heart, I'll be the first in line to rip you apart."

Carl laughed. "Your brothers being the rest of the line?"

"Damn right." Colin bunched his fists, waiting for the man's answer.

His mother slid out of the booth and stood beside Carl. "Carl suggested I hire an attorney to transfer the property into a trust." She paused and added, "In my sons' names. I haven't made up my mind."

"I don't want your ranch, Colin." Carl drew Colin's mother into his arms. "All I want is your mother. The woman I've loved since she was a girl in pigtails."

His mother's look reflected disappointment in her son. "Carl has more money than everyone in the tri-county area...put together. He doesn't want or need our ranch. I was helping him with the designs and remodeling of his home. Those were the plans I was working on with Fancy."

Colin wanted to hold onto his anger, but he couldn't. All his theories had been debunked. His mother would forgive him, and so would Carl to appease his mother.

Fancy was another story all together. Her jaw was set and her lips were pressed into a firm line. "Is that why you ran out on me this morning?"

Colin confessed, "Your cell phone went off with a text from my mother. I happened to see it."

"First of all, you had no right to read my texts."

"I know." Now he wished he'd followed his original instinct and not read the message. Only hindsight was that clear.

"Secondly, how could you believe I'd be so underhanded? Your mother has every right to do with the ranch what she wants, but I wouldn't have taken the listing unless I could tell you what was happening. I believe a relationship won't last until both parties can be open and honest with each other." Her voice broke and her bottom lip trembled.

Colin had screwed up, royally. "Fancy—"

"You should have asked." Her eyes filled. When he reached for her, she pushed past him and ran for the door.

"Fancy," he called out.

"Colin, she'd not going to listen to you now," his mother said behind him. "Go home. We'll talk when I get there."

He strode for the exit. "I have to do something."

"Trust me, Colin," Carl said. "You have to give Fancy time."

Colin turned back to the older couple. "I screwed up."

"Yes, you did." His mother held Carl's hand, her chin titled upward. "Call your brothers, tell them to meet me at the house. I have an announcement to make and I want all three of you there to hear it."

Carl lifted Maggie's hands and held them to his lips. "We'll talk later."

Colin's mother nodded.

Colin stood by, helpless to make things right. The best he could do was notify his brothers their mother wanted to see them. "Mom, I'll be at the house."

As soon as he stepped out of the diner, he dialed Brody's number, gave him the news and then dialed Angus. The men agreed to be at the house in an hour. Both wanted to know what was happening.

Colin didn't know, but he suspected his mother had come to a decision about the ranch. For their sakes, he hoped what had happened between him, Carl, Fancy and his mother hadn't destroyed his brothers' chances to keep the Rafter M.

FANCY COULD BARELY SEE through the tears in her eyes to drive back to her house, but she managed. Thankfully, traffic wasn't heavy in Temptation. She entered and went straight to her bedroom where she yanked luggage out of the closet. One by one, she emptied the drawers of her dresser into the suitcases. When one was full, she filled another with the clothes in her closet.

She'd headed for the bathroom when she caught sight of BOB on her nightstand. The tears she'd barely held in check burst like water through a broken dam, spilling onto her cheeks. The sobs rose up her throat and wracked her body with the force of her heart breaking.

Fancy fell across the bed and curled into a fetal position, crying like she had when Colin had left her the first time.

"Fancy?" a voice called out from the front of the house. "Fancy, it's me, your Uncle Carl."

"I don't want to talk to anyone," she said, her voice muffled in the pillow.

"Too bad. I'm coming in as long as you're decent."

She hugged the pillow to her chest and buried her face in it, the tears coming in another wave of misery.

"Oh, sweetheart." He sat on the edge of the bed and patted her back. "He's a man. Speaking from experience, we make stupid mistakes."

"I made the mistake," Fancy said. "I came back to Temptation to get Colin out of my system, and it backfired on me." She laughed, the sound catching on a hiccupping sob. Fancy sat up, resting her back against the padded headboard. "Joke's on me."

"Aren't we a pair?" Uncle Carl leaned back against the headboard next to her and sighed. "I came back to Temptation to get Maggie back in my life. All I've done is cause a rift between her and her sons."

"That's their problem. Those McFarlan men are all grown up. They'll get over it when they see how much you love her, and she loves you."

"I don't know." He shook his head. "I'm thinking I might have jumped the gun and pushed too hard, too fast."

"Don't give up, like me."

"You're giving up?"

Fancy flung out her hand. "What good does it do to stay here? He doesn't trust me, or my family. He thought we were taking advantage of his mother! I can't stay in Temptation. Though I admire that he wanted to protect his mother, I can't be near him when he has no respect for me. I had hoped being here would help me let go. Well, maybe it has. But I can't stay. Every time I'm near him, I would think of what could have been. It would kill me to see him moving on with his life with another woman."

Uncle Carl captured her hand. "I understand. I think we need to pack up and move back to Dallas."

"We?" She squeezed his hand. "This isn't about you and me. Just because I'm leaving doesn't mean you have to as well."

"'I can't stay when my presence is ripping Maggie's family apart." He gave her a tight smile. "But I need you to draw up the paperwork to transfer the title of my house and property to Maggie. I wanted her to help design the renovations because I'd hope to share the house with her. Now it'll have too much of her in it for me to live there without her. Let her have the house."

Fancy forgot her own misery for a moment, her

uncle's request making her stomach hurt and her heart ache. "You can't do this. Maggie loves you. It's obvious to anyone when they see the way she looks at you."

"I won't make her choose between me and her sons."

"You don't have to."

Uncle Carl patted her hand. "Just draw up the papers. I'm going back to my room to pack. I'll meet you at the diner for dinner. If you can be packed by this evening, we can leave in the morning."

"But—"

"Please," Uncle Carl interrupted. "Just do this for me."

Her chest so tight she couldn't breathe, Fancy nodded. "Okay. But you're making a big mistake."

"We're a family full of them lately, aren't we?" Her uncle left her room and exited the house, closing the front door behind him softly.

Fancy sat for a long moment, stunned by her uncle's request, wondering how she could fix this before two people who obviously loved each other were separated by the selfishness of others.

To hell with that. Pushing her own heartache aside, Fancy climbed down from the bed, grabbed her purse and headed out the door. Those McFarlan men needed a good talking to, and she was the woman to deliver it.

CHAPTER NINE

"What's this all about?" Angus asked.

Brody, Colin and Angus gathered in the living room, waiting for their mother to return home.

"Mom said she wanted us all here. She's going to make some announcement," Colin said.

"Any idea as to what she's going to say?" Brody paced the room. "Do you think she's going to back off the ultimatum and spare Colin?"

"We only had one of her boys who couldn't find a woman in her timeframe," Angus pointed out.

"Hell, he's still got time," Brody said.

Colin shook his head. "No, I don't."

"What do you mean?"

"I blew it. I thought Fancy and Carl Landers were scheming behind our backs with Mom to sell the ranch."

Angus's brows dipped. "You thought what?"

"You heard me. I guess I was looking for a reason to distrust Fancy and her uncle."

"And were they?" Brody asked.

"No." Colin shoved a hand through his hair, feeling lower than snake spit. How could he think his mother and the woman he loved would scheme to sell the ranch without telling him?

"Wow, Colin." Brody shook his head. "Way to drive off two good women." He flopped onto the couch. "I wonder what announcement Mom will make now."

"I wouldn't blame her if she kicked all of us out." Angus's jaw hardened. "In fact, I've been looking at property in the area and found a small spread I might be able to afford, if I sell some of my stock. Mom shouldn't have to worry about us anyway. This is her place. She has the right to do whatever she wants with it."

Colin nodded. "I agree. I think it's time for me to move out and find a place. I don't need much. Especially living on my own." Those words cost him. He'd had recent dreams of a house and small ranch of his own with a wife and a handful of kids—that wife being Fancy. Now that he'd blown his chances of wife and kids, he didn't need as much, and would prefer to live on his own. "Mom was right. We need to move on with our lives."

"I'm glad you boys agree with me for once." Their

mother stood at the entrance to the living room, her eyes red-rimmed and puffy, and her cheeks red and splotchy.

Colin's heart squeezed. He hadn't seen her this distraught since his father's death. "Mom, I'm sorry. I was wrong about everything."

"Damn right you were," she said, her voice hitching, her eyes narrowing at him. "Except the getting on with your lives part." She expanded her gaze to the other two men. "I see my ultimatum has caused more than its share of trouble and I withdraw it."

Colin hung his head. Whatever his mother was about to say, whatever impact it had on his brothers, this was his fault.

Brody started forward. "I wasn't happy at first, but it's the best thing that could have happened to me."

"I might not be with Gwen now, if you hadn't laid down the law, and then entered me in the cowboy auction." Angus smiled. "Like Brody said. It was the best thing that could ever happen to me."

She gave the briefest of smiles that didn't quite reach her eyes. "Let me finish."

Colin nodded. He had no words. His life hadn't improved because of the ultimatum, but it had opened his eyes to what he'd been missing and didn't even know he was missing.

Their mother pulled a large envelope from behind her back. "I'm getting rid of the ranch."

Colin could have heard a pin drop in the silence that seemed to suck the air out of the room.

He stepped forward. "It's your place. Dad left it to you. You have every right to do with it as you wish. But if you're selling because of my stupidity, don't punish Angus and Brody. I'll pack my bags and move out tonight."

She shook her head. "That won't be necessary."

Brody stepped forward. "Don't worry about me. I made enough money on the gallery showing in Dallas, I can afford a place for Jessie and me. If selling the ranch makes you happy, I'm all for it."

Angus cleared his throat. "I've been looking at acreage closer to Dallas. I found the perfect place for my horses. I can afford the payment on it. I guess what we're saying is, if you sell the place, we'll be sad, but we'll get by."

Colin swallowed, thinking of all the hard work his brothers and his parents had invested in the Rafter M. It was part of him, he couldn't hold onto it any longer. "There are lot of memories associated with this place, but they won't be lost. We will carry the memories in our hearts. And we have the rest of our lives to make new memories. We love you, Mom. We want you to be happy."

His mother's eyes filled with tears. "You are making this really hard."

Colin took his mother's hands.

Angus and Brody closed in on either side of her, touching her arms.

"We want you to be happy. If selling the ranch makes you happy, we're okay."

"I'm not selling it." She handed the packet to Angus.

"I thought you said you weren't keeping it," he said, staring down at the thick envelope.

"I'm not."

Brody chuckled. "Mom, you're not making sense."

"I'm not selling and, I'm not keeping the ranch. I'm signing it over to you three boys in a trust. It will be yours to do with as you please. I'm done with the ranch and will be moving out as soon as I find a place in town."

"What?" Colin stepped back as if he'd been sucker punched in the gut. "You can't do that."

"You just said I could do whatever I wanted with the ranch."

"But you can't leave because of me. I told you that I would leave."

"We don't expect you to give it to us. This is your home too," Colin argued. "I said I'm sorry. I meant it. Don't move out because I was a bonehead."

She patted his face. "I was planning to do this before. And you are all off the hook. You don't have to get engaged or married in my two-month timeframe. I would not have held you to it, and I would not have sold the Rafter M. I promised your father

I'd do my best to make sure the McFarlan legacy continued." She touched the envelope in Angus's hands. "I'm handing the reins to you three. It's up to you all now. Don't let your father down."

Footsteps sounded on the front deck and someone banged on the door.

"Who could that be?"

"Jessie went shopping, and she said she wouldn't be back for a couple hours. Besides she has a key," Brody said.

"Gwen and Dalton are in Dallas."

The door banged open. "Colin McFarlan!"

Colin's pulse quickened at the sound of the voice.

Fancy appeared in the entrance to the living room, her blond hair windblown, her green eyes flashing. "Colin, you better fix things before it's too late."

He held up his hands, hope filling his chest. "I would, if I knew how."

"Well, Mr. Smartypants, you have my uncle packing his bags as we speak."

"Why?"

"He thinks he's coming between you, your brothers and your mother." Fancy marched across the floor and poked her finger into his chest. "My uncle is a good man. He doesn't want your stinking ranch or money. He's in love with your mother and wants her to be happy. He's going to leave rather than come between all of you."

Colin's mother pressed a hand to her chest, tears spilling from her eyes. "Are you sure he still wants me?"

Fancy's voice softened as she addressed the McFarlan matriarch. "He's so in love with you he asked me to sign the house he's been renovating over to you, because he couldn't stand to live there, seeing you in everything and you not being there to enjoy it with him. He wanted you to help design the transformation, because it was to be your house as much as his."

Angus and Brody frowned at Colin. "We have to make this right."

Colin stared at his mother. "I'm going to fix this. I promise."

She shook her head. "I don't see how."

"I'm going to talk to Carl." Collin started for the door. "I'll make him see that I was wrong."

More footsteps clumped across the deck, a loud knock sounded on the front door and then the door banged open. "Maggie!"

Colin's mother's eyes widened. "Carl?"

Carl Landers stepped into the living room, his gaze finding Colin's mother. "I've been thinking and I've come to a conclusion."

Her lips quirked. "You have?"

He frowned. "Yes, I have." Then as if noticing the three men for the first time, he pointed to each, one at a time. "John McFarlan was a good man and a good father. I know he raised you all to be responsible and look out for your mother. I admire that and understand why you would be suspicious of any man who came into her life."

"I was wrong about you," Colin interrupted.

Carl nodded. "But for the right reasons. You didn't know my intentions and you should have been leery. I'm telling you now." He took a deep breath and focused on Maggie as he spoke. "I want to make your mother happy. I don't give a flying flip for your ranch. I don't want your money. I have more than I can spend in my lifetime."

He stepped up to Colin's mother. "I want you to be happy." Reaching for her hands, he lifted them and held them against his chest. "If me leaving Temptation makes you happy, I will. But I couldn't until I told you how I felt."

He stared down into her eyes. "I've loved you since you were that cute gangly teen in pigtails. I loved you when we used to hang out together with John, the fearsome threesome. I regret I didn't ask you to marry me before John did and I came back to Temptation for a second chance."

He dropped to one knee. "Maggie, I love you with all my heart. If you and your sons think there is any chance in hell you'd agree to marry me, I'd like for you to give me the chance to prove to you that I can make you happy."

Their mother's tears trickled down her cheeks as

she stared at the man on his knee. Then she turned her gaze to her three sons.

Colin spoke first. "If you love him, say yes!"

"You don't need our approval," Brody reasoned.

"But we give it," Angus offered.

"Wholeheartedly," Colin concluded. "Any man who loves our mother enough to brave pissing off her three sons has to be strong enough to take care of her."

"And if you don't…" Angus's eyes narrowed, "…we know where you live."

Carl looked up at Maggie. "Seems they approve. Do you?"

Maggie's lips curled into a smile, the grin spreading across her face. "Yes."

"Yes, you approve? Or yes, you'll give me a chance?"

She pulled him to his feet. "Yes, I'll marry you."

Carl laughed and pulled her into his arms. "Thank you. Oh, Maggie, I love you so much, I couldn't leave without knowing how you felt."

"I love you too." She leaned back. "I loved John and I'll miss him the rest of my life, but I love you too. I have enough room in my heart."

Colin's heart swelled at his mother's happiness. But his life was still in shambles. He glanced at Fancy who was watching the proposal unfold with tears in her eyes.

Like Carl, he had to know, one way or another, if

he stood a chance of Fancy forgiving him for being a putz. And if she'd ever let him close enough to make it up to her, hopefully for the rest of their lives.

He stepped past his mother and Carl hugging and kissing in the middle of the room, captured Fancy's hand and led her out of the house. When he started down the porch steps, she hesitated. He held her hand. "Please walk with me."

Her eyes narrowed. For a moment Colin thought she'd refuse, but then she stepped down beside him.

"I'm still mad at you."

"And you have every right to be."

"I guess what Uncle Carl said put it in perspective. You three McFarlan brothers were looking out for your mother. I can understand why you would be upset if you thought someone was taking advantage of her."

They'd walked past the barn and stopped at the wooden fence rails overlooking the pasture where Angus kept some of his best horses.

Colin lifted the hand he'd been holding and threaded his fingers with hers. "I was wrong to accuse you of keeping secrets from me. I should have known better and I'll understand if you never forgive me. But I'd really like you to give me a second chance. That one night together, even though it was bad timing, let me know that you were the one for me. No other woman measured up to you. When everything fell apart eight years ago, I should have come after you. It took me eight years to realize why I couldn't find a woman to love. I was already in love."

"How do I know you won't love me today and ditch me tomorrow?"

"I give you my word, my heart and all of my love." He brought her hand to his lips. "Will you forgive me and give me another chance?"

"I didn't want to fall in love with you again," she said. "And I didn't."

Colin's heart dropped to his belly. He'd tried, and failed.

Her eyes brightened, a smile slipping across her face. "Because I never *stopped* loving you," she whispered.

"And all those women I dated and dropped...were because none of them captured my heart. Like you did. I love you, Fancy. I want to marry you and have a handful of children."

"Is that a proposal?"

"It will be once I get down on one knee." Before Colin could drop to one knee, Fancy flung her arms around his neck.

"Yes! I will marry you."

"Good, because I just noticed a cow pile where I would have put my knee." He gathered her in his arms and kissed her.

Colin couldn't think of anywhere he'd rather be,

or anyone he'd rather love. Life was turning out pretty good.

***If you enjoyed this book, try the other books in the
Ugly Stick Saloon Series***

Boots & Chaps (#1)
Boots & Sex Ed (#2)
Boots & Leather (#3)
Boots & Promises (#4)
Boots & Bareback (#5)
Boots & Dirty Tricks (#6)
Boots & Lace (#7)
Boots & Roses (#8)
Boots & Buckles (#9)
Boots & the Wishes (#10)
Boots & Twisters (#11)
Boots & the Bachelor (#12)
Boots & The Rogue (#13)
Boots & The Heartbreaker (#14)
Boots & Wings (#15)

BOOTS & WINGS

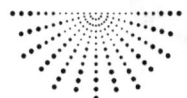

UGLY STICK SALOON SERIES BOOK #15

by Elle James
New York Times Bestselling Author

writing as

Myla Jackson

BOOTS
&
WINGS

UGLY STICK SALOON

New York Times Bestselling Au...
ELLE JAMES
writing as
MYLA JACKSON

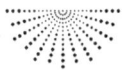

"*D*id you lock and secure the plane and helicopter?" Tucker Maddox asked from behind his sturdy metal desk.

His brother, Jake, carried his flight bag through the door. The heat and dust of the Texas summer followed him inside. "Done. Buttoned up, secure and fueled up for tomorrow."

"Good." Tucker closed his logbook. "Maybe we'll get out of here early today."

Jake stretched his arms over his head. "We deserve a little rest and relaxation after two weeks of non-stop gigs. Oh, and my last client tipped me a hundred dollars. The beer's on me at the Ugly Stick Saloon tonight."

Tucker cocked his brows. "You have a five a.m. flight in the morning. Should you be drinking tonight?"

Jake shook his head. "What's one beer gonna hurt? After the month we've had, we deserve a little fun."

"It's only been really bad the past two weeks."

"My point exactly." Jake shoved his flight gear onto the shelf behind the customer counter. "Besides, I think it's ladies night. By the time we get *cleaned* up, they'll be *liquored* up and ready for some Maddox lovin'."

"Can't you wait for that beer until we go to Nick's bachelor party? Audrey promised a hot stripper for the event and she's closing the saloon for us after eleven. Should be a good time."

"That's next weekend. I want a beer and good company now." Jake dropped into his chair, kicked up his heels, plunked them onto his desk and leaned back with his hands behind his neck. "I can't believe Nick's taking the plunge. Do you suppose it's because he's over thirty and starting to feel his age?"

"Hey." Tucker frowned. "I'm over thirty, and you'll be thirty in four months."

Jake closed his eyes and stretched again. "Don't tell me you've been thinking about settling down and raising a family."

Over the past month, working as much as he had, Tucker had been thinking just that. He wasn't getting any younger, and he didn't want to be alone all his life. When he'd left the army four years ago, he'd put relationships on hold until he got his affairs in order.

He and Jake started the business, almost going bankrupt in the first year.

Thankfully the business kept Tucker from dwelling on his past. Coming off active duty, he'd been plagued by nightmares of his days and nights as a Black Hawk helicopter pilot. Over time, the dreams had dissipated. He'd weaned himself off sleep aids a year ago and hadn't taken them since. Lately, instead of dreaming about RPG attacks and evacuating wounded warriors, a feisty female haunted his dreams, making him wake up in the middle of the night. Not yelling, thrashing and reliving a nightmare, but aroused, hard and ready for lovemaking.

Going home to the small ranch he and his brother had inherited from their parents was okay, but it would be a whole lot better with a woman to warm his bed. And not just any woman. Molly O'Brien.

The youngest of the O'Brien clan, Molly had been a pigtailed pest tagging along behind her brothers when Tucker was in high school. But the girl had since grown up. The beautiful spitfire hit every one of the requirements on his list.

Smart, beautiful, loved kids and she had a heart as big as the state of Texas.

"I have to admit, with Nick's bachelor party coming up, it got me thinking along those lines as well," Jake said.

Tucker snorted. "Like you could settle for one

female when there is...what do you call it...oh yes, a smorgasbord of women to choose from."

Jake shrugged. "In case you haven't noticed, the pickin's are getting slimmer the older we get. Nick's marrying Lacey. Audrey and Jackson Gray Wolf hooked up and are expecting their first kid. Libby's with Jackson's brothers, Mark and Luke. Connor Mason snagged Kendall, and rodeo champion, Grant Raleigh, took Mona off the market—"

Tucker raised his hand. "Okay, okay. I get it. We're running out of options. But that doesn't mean we have to hurry out and propose to the first unattached female we find."

"No, but if we don't move quickly on the ones we like, we may get beat out by someone else."

Tucker crossed his arms and stared across the desk at his younger brother. "So, what are you going to do about it?"

Jake raked a hand through his thick, black hair, making it stand on end. "I never thought I'd say this, but I think it's time I got hitched."

"Just like that?"

His brother shrugged. "I'm not getting any younger."

"You're twenty-nine, not an old man. Got someone in mind?" Tucker waited for his answer. Jake had been out with nearly every woman in the tri-county area. For him to settle on one was a big deal.

"I don't know. I've only been out with one lady more than once. She's sassy, sexy and independent enough she could put up with the type of work we're in. She loves the outdoors as much as I do, and she's not clingy." He smiled and gazed at the wall as if he were seeing the woman in front of him. "She's got one helluva great body, and kisses like nobody's business. I really think I'm in love with her." He glanced up at his brother. "I'm sure she's the one for me."

Tucker snapped his fingers, urging his brother to get to the point. "Name?"

"You know her. Hell, you've gone out with her a few times yourself." He grinned. "Molly O'Brien."

Lead sank to the pit of Tucker's belly, and his jaw tightened. "Sorry, she's taken."

Jake shot a frown toward his brother. "Well, damn. Did I miss something? Who snuck in and claimed her?"

Tucker stood, pushing his chair back so hard it hit the wall. "Me."

Jake's brows wrinkled. "You? When did you pop the question? Hell, I'm your brother. You could have at least consulted me before you did."

Tucker pulled at the collar of his Maddox Air Charter Service polo shirt and looked away from his brother's gaze. "It's not official yet."

"What do you mean it's not official?"

"Well…" Tucker's cheeks burned, "I haven't actually asked her. I planned to take her out over the next couple weeks, get to know her even better and let her get to know me. Then I'll pop the question."

Jake's frown lifted and his face split into a smile. "You haven't asked her?" He slapped his cowboy hat against his thigh. "Whew! And I thought she was a goner." He stood and plunked his hat on his head. "As far as I'm concerned, she's fair game until she says yes."

Tucker's eyes narrowed. "I've had my eye on Molly longer than you. Don't get in the way of my courtship."

Jake laughed out loud. "Listen to yourself. You sound like a man from the eighteen hundreds. Molly is young, daring and adventurous. Why would she marry a stick in the mud like you?"

"Any woman would be happy to marry a man who's stable, caring and treats her like she's special."

Jake yawned. "Boring."

Tucker slammed his fist onto the desk. "Damn it, Jake! This isn't a game or sporting event like when we were in high school competing against each other. I care about Molly. I'd go so far as to say, I'm in love with her."

"So am I." Jake's shoulders straightened, and he stared hard at Tucker. "I care enough to let her choose who she wants to be with. We both have a shot at winning her heart. We can date her and let her get to know both of us. After two weeks, she can make her choice and the one she doesn't choose has to back off."

Tucker thought about it for a minute. Molly was pretty independent-minded and would make her own decision. He just had to convince her to choose him. "Two weeks might not be enough for her to decide."

"Then we'll reevaluate at the end of the two weeks and extend the deadline if that's what it takes." Jake stepped up to his brother. "So for the next two weeks, we'll *both* date the pretty Molly O'Brien without interfering with each other's attempts to win her over." He stuck out his hand. "Deal?"

Not convinced this was a good idea, Tucker didn't have much choice. He took his brother's hand and shook on it. "Deal."

"Now, let's get out of here. I have some errands to run and then there's a beer with my name on it at the Ugly Stick."

"And I have some accounts to take care of back at the ranch." Tucker fully intended to ignore the accounts. To win Molly's heart, he had to get to her before his brother. If he wasn't mistaken, she worked at the Ugly Stick Saloon that night. He'd have to be there before Jake and stake his claim on the pretty lady, to let her know he was interested in long-term commitment.

Jake was as charming as a snake-oil salesman and could talk a girl out of her panties in the blink of an eye. Tucker would have his work cut out for him if he wanted Molly to fall for him.

* * *

"MOLLY!"

Molly O'Brien had just pulled on her boots and her cowboy hat after arriving home from a quick trip to town for groceries. "What do you need, Gabe?" she called out to her brother.

"Have you seen Isabella?" his voice came to her from the hallway.

Molly shook her head and smiled. "She's probably out at the barn with her horse."

"I checked. She and her horse were gone." Gabe stopped in front of Molly's bedroom door. "Where are you going?"

"It's hot outside. I've spent the best part of my day pushing a shopping cart through the grocery store, and I'm ready to blow the cobwebs out of my hair."

"Going riding, huh?" Gabe nodded. "That's what Isabella does when she's all wound up. What's got your chaps in a twist?"

"Nothing. Everything."

Gabe grinned. "You're talking like a female. Didn't we teach you better?" He crossed his arms over his chest and leaned against the doorframe. "Spill."

She shrugged and stood, stomping her foot to get it

the rest of the way into her boot. "I'm twenty-seven years old, I have a degree in marketing, I work at a saloon and I haven't gotten laid in the past six months. Either things better change around here soon, or I'm heading for Austin to find a job and men my age to date."

"There are plenty of men in Temptation who'd love to date you," Gabe said.

Molly lifted her chin. "Yeah? Name one."

"What about Nick...No, wait...I'm going to his bachelor party next week." Gabe scratched his jaw and frowned. "How about Grant Raleigh? He's a champion rodeo rider."

"Taken," Molly said. "Try again."

Gabe lifted two fingers. "Mark or Luke Gray Wolf."

"In a relationship with Libby Jones."

Gabe frowned. "Trent Jameson."

"He and Isaac are with Lucky Albright."

"Well damn, Molly. You're not trying hard enough." Gabe turned and led the way toward the kitchen. "There are more men around than that."

"I'm running out of options, and I'm not settling for some toothless old goat because I'm desperate." Molly's lips twisted. Not even a toothless old goat had asked her out in the last couple of weeks.

Gabe draped an arm around her shoulder. "I don't expect you to *settle* for anyone. Especially not an old goat."

"Well, in case you haven't noticed, the good ones aren't beating down my door to ask me out.

Gabe stepped back and stared at Molly in her jeans and tank top. "Why not? You're all right for a girl."

She snorted. "Thanks. I think."

"You know what I mean." Gabe scratched his head. "You being my baby sister and all."

Molly tilted her head, considering her dilemma. "I think the guys might be intimidated by my heavy-handed brothers."

"Whose heavy-handed brothers?" Sean entered the kitchen through the back door, followed by Tanner, his arm wrapped around Isabella's waist.

With three of the four hulking O'Brien men in the kitchen, it didn't leave Molly much room to move, much less think.

"Are you boys being overprotective again?" Isabella asked. She left Tanner's side and closed the distance between her and Molly. "Molly's a grown woman. She can take care of herself."

"What are you talking about?" Tanner asked. "She's just a kid."

"I'm twenty-seven. A year younger than Isabella."

Isabella slipped an arm around Molly and hugged her close. "She's fully capable of making her own decisions about men."

Molly smiled at Isabella's defense and gave a curt nod to her brothers. "That's right."

Sean frowned. "What if one of them tries to hurt her?"

"Yeah." Gabe's chest swelled. "We promised Dad we'd look out for our little sister. Speaking of Dad, he'd kick our asses if he comes home from his trip to Australia to find his baby girl moved out."

"First of all, if someone tries to hurt me, I'll take him down with one of the moves you taught me," Molly said. "Second. Dad isn't coming home for another month, what he doesn't know won't hurt him. Besides, you boys are too big for Dad to kick your asses."

Gabe's brows crooked upward. "You've seen him when he gets mad."

Molly shook her head. "The point is, I haven't been asked out on a date for a while. It might just be time for me to move on and make a life of my own away from Temptation where everyone knows everyone else."

"But Austin is such a big city," Gabe said.

"It's full of crime," Sean added.

Tanner frowned. "And far away."

"It's not as far as where Jesse lives," Molly pointed out.

Gabe's frown deepened. "Don't even think of running off to New York."

"I'm not going that far. Yet. But I *am* going to Austin, just as soon as I find a job. I've updated my resume, and I've signed up with a headhunter. It's time I grew up and got a life of my own."

All three of her brothers spoke at once, the combined noise too much to make any sense.

Molly raised her hand. "Don't bother trying to talk me out of it. I need to do this for me. There's nothing in Temptation holding me back." And no one begging her to stay.

"What about us?" Sean asked. "Don't you care about us?"

With a gentle smile for her brother, Molly touched his cheek. "I love you all, and Isabella too. You know how happy I am you've found each other. Seeing your loving relationship only makes me feel more alone."

"You're not alone," Tanner said. "You have us."

Molly shook her head. "You missed the part about my not having gotten laid in the past six months."

Tanner pressed his hands over his ears. "I did not want to know that."

"That I haven't been laid? Or that I'm not a virgin?" She backhanded him in the belly, forcing him to drop his hands.

"Either." Tanner closed his eyes. "I can't see my baby sister in bed with a man." He shook his head and glanced at her. "Sorry. I'll always see you as a ten-year-old."

"Exactly." She stared around at three of her four brothers. "As long as you three are around, I'll be an old maid. I'm giving Audrey my notice tonight. I'm giving myself two weeks to find a job, and then I'm out of here." She marched toward the door, pushing past Tanner.

"Wait!" Tanner snagged her arm. "What about those fly boys, Jake and Tucker Maddox?"

"Yeah," Sean said. "They aren't too old."

Her footsteps faltered at the thought of the Maddox brothers. Yeah, she liked them all right, had even thought she might be falling in love with them. She'd gone out several times with each and enjoyed the dates immensely, but neither had called her in more than two weeks. "What about them?" she hedged.

"I thought you liked one of them," Tanner said.

Sean added, "They're single."

Gabe grinned. "Best of all they're young, and have all of their teeth."

"Huh?" Tanner looked at his brother.

Gabe waved his hand. "Never mind. You ought to be able to catch one of the Maddox brothers."

Molly shook her head. "They aren't fish. I'm not going to throw a line in the water and snag one of them."

Isabella chuckled and rolled her eyes. "Molly, sweetie, good luck with these three poor excuses for matchmakers. I'm going to get a shower." She hugged her. "If you need an ear to vent in, come see me later."

Molly gave Isabella a grateful glance. "Thanks, Bella."

Fortunately all three of her brothers' attention swerved to their departing love, as Bella left the kitchen.

"Well, uh, I'm sure you'll figure it all out," Sean said to Molly, his gaze on Isabella's swaying hips.

"Yeah, Isabella's right—you're old enough to make your own decisions." Tanner pushed past Sean on his way after Isabella.

"Hey!" Sean grabbed his brother's arm and hauled him back. "The shower's only big enough for two."

"I know," Tanner said. "Isabella is one. I'm the two."

"Like hell you are." The two wrestled each other out of the kitchen and bumped into the walls down the hallway.

"I'm taking my shower alone," Isabella called out from the back of the house.

The men stopped fighting.

"What about after?" Sean asked.

"We'll see," Isabella's voice faded away.

Gabe pulled Molly into one of his big bear hugs. "Just don't rush into leaving. We love you and would like you to stay close to family. We've already lost one of us to the lure of the big city. We'd hate to lose you as well."

Molly squeezed her brother around the middle, burying her face in his shirt, loving the scent of the outdoors that reminded her so much of her father. "You didn't lose Jesse. He's alive and well, riding his horse for the New York City Police Department. And he's happy with the love of his life." She leaned back in her brother's arms and stared up at him. "That's all I want—to be happy with the love of my life."

Her brother tweaked her nose like he had when she'd been an eight-year-old. "I get that. But give the men of the area a chance before you bail on the ranch and us. That's all we're asking."

Molly sighed. "I'll give it until I find a job I can make a living at in Austin. If nothing happens by then, I'm packing my bags."

"Fair enough." He let his arms fall to his sides.

Molly nodded toward the hallway where Isabella, Sean and Tanner had disappeared. "You better hurry. The boys will wear her out before you get to her."

Gabe winked. "I can wait."

"Maybe you can, but can she?" Molly laughed. "I don't know how you four make it work."

Her brother ran a hand through his hair. "I don't either, but somehow it does. Who'd have thought the three of us could share one woman and not kill each other?"

Molly smiled, shaking her head. "I'm happy for you. Isabella is special. Don't screw it up." She left Gabe in the kitchen and headed out to the barn.

Little Joe stood at the pasture fence, waiting for her, stomping his hoof.

"You are so spoiled." Molly dug a carrot out of her pocket and held it out for the horse. She had to stop bringing carrots, apples and sugar cubes when she visited the barn. Little Joe had come to expect a treat every time.

She led the gelding into the barn, brushed and saddled him, and slipped a bridle over his head. By the time she was finished, he was dancing excitedly, as ready as she was to race across the pasture, letting the wind blow in his ears.

Outside the barn, Molly stepped into the stirrup and slung her leg over the saddle. She hadn't even gotten her foot in the other stirrup before Little Joe took off.

Laughing out loud, she let go of her worries, leaning over the horse's neck. She loved the feel of the hot sun's rays beating down on her back and the big, blue hazy sky of a Texas summer stretching above her.

Little Joe galloped across the fields, down into the valleys and up over the knolls, headed for his and Molly's favorite place in the whole world—the bend in the creek where a pool had formed. The place her parents brought her and her brothers when they were little and taught them to swim.

It was the one place on the entire ranch where she felt the most relaxed and comfortable. Away from everything and everyone, she could really think through her options...or not think at all.

Little Joe arrived at the creek, breathing hard, his coat lathered with sweat.

Molly swung off his back and dropped to the ground. She led the horse to the water and he drank, pulling gulp after of gulp into his mouth. When he was satisfied, he wandered toward a shady patch of grass where he happily munched.

Oh to be so easily satisfied. Molly sighed, toed off her boots and sat on a boulder at the pool's edge, dangling her feet in the cool water, watching the ripples spread out across the surface.

Gabe's words came back to her.

What about the Maddox brothers?

That was a question she had posed to herself a dozen times. She'd been around them for years, hanging out at the Ugly Stick Saloon. They'd danced together, and partied when the saloon had special events. Tucker and Jake were brothers, but as different as night and day.

Tucker was the levelheaded, sweet and considerate man a girl could see herself marrying. Oh, and he was an excellent kisser, and his slow, steady foreplay stirred her insides to the point where she'd wanted to strip naked and push him out of that sweet comfort zone. He'd only gone to second base, feeling up her breasts before he'd stepped away and ended the evenings they'd spent together. He wanted her to be sure about them before they went any further.

Yeah, he was sweet, and those big, rough hands...*Wowza*.

Now, Jake was the kind of man mamas warned their daughters about, and daddies stood at the front door with their shotguns to keep away. He made her core ignite. One of the dates she'd been on with him had ended abruptly when her brother, Tanner, drove up behind them at Lookout Point and put the kibosh on a backseat quickie. Yeah, her brothers had a habit of showing up at the wrong time.

And what killed her was that the dates had stopped a couple weeks ago. Neither Jake nor Tucker had called to claim another. And maybe that was a good thing. At some point, she'd have to choose between the two of them and she wasn't so sure she could.

Both men were professional pilots, driven in their desire to make their business work for them, and still cowboys at heart. She loved that about them and she was so close to falling in love with both of them, it scared her.

The thought of the two men made the day warmer to the point Molly pulled her tank top out of the waistband of her jeans and flapped the hem to stir up a breeze against her heated skin.

"Oh, what the heck." She yanked the shirt over her head and dropped it beside her on the boulder. The cool, clear water below beckoned. Within seconds, she'd shucked the rest of her clothes down to the bathing suit she'd been born with.

Deliciously naked, she dove into the water, the cool liquid caressing her hot body, bringing her outer temperature down while her core flamed. Nothing was better than skinny-dipping unless it was skinny-dipping with a really hot guy.

ABOUT THE AUTHOR

Twenty years of livin' and lovin' on a South Texas ranch raising horses, cattle, goats, ostriches and emus left an indelible impression on Myla Jackson, one she likes to instill in her red-hot stories. Myla pens wildly sexy, fun adventures of all genres including historical westerns, medieval tales, romantic suspense, contemporary romance and paranormal beasties of all shapes and sexy sizes. She lives in the tree-covered hills of Northwest Arkansas with her husband of more than 20 years and her muses—the human-wanna-be canines—Chewy and Sweetpea.

To learn more about Myla Jackson and her alter ego Elle James visit:
www.mylajackson.com
mylajackson@mylajackson.com

ALSO BY MYLA JACKSON

Trouble with Mitch

Bound and Tied

Honor Bound

Duty Bound

River Bound

Paranormal

Shewolf

Thorn's Kiss

Sex, Lies & Vampire Hunters